"He wants me to come home for the summer.

I practically slammed on the brakes. "Get serious."

"My grandfather is getting old and wants to teach me things before he dies. Customs, traditions, rituals—the Navaho Way. My grandfather never did like the idea of my going away. He thought I should have stayed with my mother's people. Obviously my dad disagreed."

"Well, you *can't* go back this summer," I said. "You're going to be in New York City."

"Come on, Marcus. New York is a long shot." Henry shifted in his seat. "I haven't even started writing the essay yet about the me nobody knows."

For some reason I found myself getting very angry with Henry's father. He hardly wrote anymore. As far as I was concerned, he barely existed. Now suddenly he was showing up in Henry's life, making demands.

And for some funny reason I started feeling pretty irritated with Henry too. He should have just laughed and made some sort of joke when he read the letter, he should have crumpled it up into a little ball. He should have stuffed it into an ashtray, just to show how stupid the idea of returning to the reservation was.

Diana closed the book she'd been reading. I could tell she was interested in our conversation.

"I think you ought to consider going home for a while, Henry," she said.

"*What?* Are you nuts?"

===

A. E CANNON's first novel, *Cal Cameron by Day, Spider-Man™ by Night*, won the Fifth Annual Delacorte Press Prize for an Outstanding First Young Adult Novel. She lives with her husband and sons and their many pets in Salt Lake City.

The Shadow Brothers

A. E. Cannon

LAUREL-LEAF BOOKS

Published by
Dell Publishing
a division of
Bantam Doubleday Dell Publishing Group, Inc.
666 Fifth Avenue
New York, New York 10103

ISBN: 0-440-21167-0

RL: 5.0

Reprinted by arrangement with Delacorte Press

Printed in the United States of America

February 1992

10 9 8 7 6 5 4 3 2 1

RAD

For my own brothers,
John and Jimmy

1

THE HEARSE WAS HENRY'S IDEA.

Last summer—right before our junior year—
Henry and I decided to buy a car, which was fine with
my parents as long as we bought the car with our own
money and then took care of everything once we got
it. And I do mean *everything*—gas, taxes, insurance.
But we decided to go for it anyway. Who cares if we
had to sell popcorn and take tickets at the Camelot
Theater for the rest of our lives? A car, we figured, was
worth it. If only we could find one cheap.

Enter the hearse.

It was a Saturday afternoon. Henry found me in
the balcony of the Camelot with a broom. A lady in the
audience complained that a bat was buzzing her head
like a small jet fighter, so Fritz, our fearless leader and
theater manager, pulled me from behind the concession stand and ordered me to go upstairs with a broom.

"A broom, Fritz?" I said. "A *broom*? What do you
want me to do with a broom? Find the bat and ask it to
please clean up after itself?"

"Oh, very funny, creep," Fritz barked. "Ve-ry funny!" Fritz is in his late twenties. He has a crewcut and large mutant-type biceps. *The Terminator,* which he has seen 237 times, is his favorite movie. "Here's what I want you to do. I want you to take this broom and terrorize the little vampire. Then, after you've done that for a while, I want you to kill, kill, kill it until it's completely dead. *Comprendo,* soldier boy?"

"Kill until dead," I said. "Right." I took the broom and left. The whole problem with Fritz, I thought to myself, is that the only two things he ever reads are *Soldier of Fortune* and *Reader's Digest.* No wonder the man is seriously warped.

So that's why Henry found me in the balcony of Camelot Theater with a broom.

"Why are you waving that broom in the air, Marcus?" Henry asked when he saw me.

"I'm trying to attract a bat for Fritz."

"Fritz wants a bat?"

"Yeah," I told him, "for dinner."

Henry laughed. Henry always laughs at my jokes. It's one of the things I like best about him.

Let me explain. Henry is Henry Yazzie, my Navaho foster brother. We're the same age, and he's lived with my family here in Lake View, Utah, since he was seven years old. Henry is one of the smartest guys you'll ever meet, but he isn't weird about how brilliant he is. He isn't the kind of guy, for example, who would ever spend his time swapping SAT scores with you or trying to access the school district's records with his personal computer. Henry likes regular stuff like hanging around, looking at girls, watching sports on

TV. Did I also mention he runs? Henry is one of the best high-school distance runners in the entire state of Utah.

There is one thing a little different about him, though. Henry writes poems. But he's quiet, almost *secretive*, about it. He writes poems the way a cat would write a poem—that is, if cats could write. Henry just watches everything going on around him through narrowed eyes, and then he writes when no one is looking. Hardly anybody knows about Henry's poems except for me and our English teacher, Miss Brett, whom I personally believe was one of Shakespeare's original role models for the witches in *Macbeth*. I don't even think my mom, who is a big-time Henry fan, knows about his notebook full of poems. Maybe the fact that Henry writes poems says something about his ability to see things (like hearses) in a new and usually improved light.

Generally Henry and I worked the same shift at Camelot Theater, but today I was covering for one of the other guys, which is why I had the very great privilege of waving brooms at enemy bats while Henry watched.

"How'd you get in?" I asked.

"Crazy Smitty let me in through the back."

"Then it's Crazy Smitty's rear if Fritz catches you. Not mine. Okay?"

"Fine," said Henry. He pulled a folded section of newspaper from his back pocket, then sat down and draped his long runner's legs over the edge of the balcony. "I think I just may have found us a car."

"Serious?"

"Yeah," said Henry. "Here's what it says. 'MUST SEE TO BELIEVE! Black sedan. Roomy. Will consider any offer.'"

"Any offer?" I said. "Sounds interesting."

"I called already," Henry said. "The guy said we could come out this afternoon. What time do you get off?"

"Four," I said.

"Great. I'll pick you up."

"I'll still be in uniform," I warned him. Fritz makes us wear maroon velveteen jackets with black pants and mailman shoes. Also, we have to wear white shirts and high cardboard collars with black bow ties. But, hey, what can I say. I love looking like Jerry Lewis.

Henry was waiting for me in front of the theater at four o'clock. He was driving Dad's old Chevy. I don't know. You'd think Dad, who makes good money as a shrink, would drive something a little classier, a little flashier. A BMW, for example. I crawled into the passenger seat. Henry turned on the radio, raced through the stations until he found Rock 103, and took off.

As it turned out, the guy with the black sedan lived clear on the other side of town, down by the lake, in a little house done up in aluminum siding. His front yard was filled with old tires, a picnic table, and a flock of geese. Real ones—not plastic. And oh, yeah. There was a car in the driveway. It was big. It was black. It had heavy curtains. And it was definitely a hearse.

Henry and I looked at it.

I couldn't believe it. "Do you think this is it? The roomy black sedan?"

A slow grin was spreading across Henry's face. "I'll just bet it is."

"It's a hearse, Henry," I said.

"So it is," he said.

"A hearse."

Henry started to laugh.

"I want a *car*," I said. "I want a Camaro. A red one with front and rear spoilers and a T-top so that I and my many dates can feel the wind in our hair when we drive through town on warm summer nights. Henry, I want a car that girls will go to dances in. As a rule girls don't ride in hearses unless they're dead."

"Marcus," Henry said, "this has definite potential. Think of this hearse as a highly specialized luxury car—"

"A sort of stretch limo for stiffs?" I said. "Well, now, *that* makes me feel a whole lot better."

I looked at the hearse.

"Can't you see it?" Henry was saying. "You and me in dark sunglasses, cruising town in this thing? I'll be Dr. Doom and you'll be my loyal henchman."

I started to smile to myself. The picture of Henry and me behind the wheel—well, it did have a certain appeal.

"Yeah," I said. Then I laughed too. "Why do I always let you talk me into things? Let's find out what the guy wants for it."

The guy was a fifty-year-old man with a huge stomach that hung out over a belt buckle that said COORS.

He'd inherited the hearse from his brother, whom he happened to hate.

"Do I look dead to you?" he screamed at us.

"Not yet," said Henry.

"Then what the hell do I need a hearse for?" He kept screaming and spraying spit all over us. *"I ain't taking a ride in one of them things until I've got a tag on my toe. Know what I mean?"*

We nodded.

He accepted our offer and threw in the drapes for free.

The next day Henry and I took a bus to the lake and picked it up. On the way home we stopped at a little place that sells magazines and posters, and we bought a bumper sticker that said FROM 0 TO 60 IN 15 MINUTES. Henry stuck it on the rear bumper.

My parents, my little sister, Julia, and our neighbor, Diana Rogers, were sitting on the front porch playing with Diana's old dog Boston when we pulled up. I wish you could have seen all their faces.

"Ooofer gross!" Julia yelled. "You guys are total perverts."

Diana's mouth fell wide open. My mother and father got up slowly and started walking across the lawn toward us. I think they may have been in a state of semishock.

"So what do you think, Boss?" Henry asked Dad. Henry always calls him "Boss."

"Speechless" pretty well describes my parents right then. Henry went on.

"Please feel free to take it anytime, Boss"—

Henry's smile got bigger —"but you are strictly forbidden to change the radio station."

Dad loves country-western music, which Henry hates.

By now Mom and Dad had walked across the lawn. They were standing nose to nose with the hearse.

"You know all those things people say about the children of psychiatrists?" Dad said, putting his arm around Mom's shoulders.

"That they're antisocial and maladjusted?" Henry said.

Dad nodded. "I'm beginning to think that they're all true."

THAT WAS ALMOST A YEAR AGO.

I was thinking about Henry today because I was cleaning our room after I got home from the bus depot, and I found an essay he wrote this spring. It was on the floor, under the desk, crumpled into a neat paper ball. He'd aimed for the garbage can and missed. The ball had rolled under the desk and stayed there until now.

I don't even know why I bothered to smooth the ball out and read it. Reading garbage is not a favorite hobby of mine, but I recognized Henry's handwriting on the outside. Henry's handwriting is so beautiful, you might almost think it belongs to a girl—except there's something strong about it too. It looks Gothic.

The paper turned out to be an essay called "The Me Nobody Knows." I even remembered the day he wrote it—and threw it away. I sat down on the edge of the bed and I read it for the very first time.

Would you believe me, Henry wrote, *if I told you this valley belonged to Indians once?*

All of it. There were no malls then, no foreign-car dealerships, no video arcades, no gas stations, no movie theaters, no college on the hill. There wasn't even a McDonald's. Just the lake to the west, mountains to the east, and a valley floor between, covered with long grasses that hissed in the canyon breezes like snakes. And of course there were the Indians.

The Utes used to roam this valley. Fierce, bold, clever—they made life miserable for the Paiutes to the south, who grubbed their lives away in dirty hovels. The Utes raided Paiute villages and took their children captive and sold them as slaves to the Spanish. Then they rode home again with stars screaming overhead and the wind howling at their backs like wolves.

The white men who came here—first the Catholics and then the Mormons—changed all that. They fought with the Utes and sometimes converted them to Christianity and finally sent the rest to reservations in northeastern Utah. And now all that's left is a high school named after one of the last, one of the greatest Utes, Chief Wakara.

Wakara High School, where the students are white and occasionally Hispanic—except for me. I am Native American and sometimes when I wake in the middle of the night, emerge from my cave of dreams, I think I am a symbol. I am a symbol of how complete the white man's victory was here.

I put the paper down when I was finished. The Henry no one knew. Not even the people who loved him. That must have hurt him most of all, I think, the fact that I—*me* of all people—couldn't see how things must have been for him.

I took the essay, and I folded it carefully in half. Then I folded it in half again and again and placed it safely in the corner of my top drawer.

Maybe if I'd read it sooner I would have understood. I would have seen what was coming. Maybe and maybe not.

Sometimes, people—they just don't want to see.

2

I MAKE A LOT OF LISTS.

I make them on paper. I make them in my head. I especially make them when I'm bored. And since I am usually bored in English, I make a lot of lists there. It's great. The teacher, Miss Brett, thinks I'm taking notes like crazy. The only thing she can't figure out is why a guy who takes as many notes as I do keeps failing her tests. Miss Brett thinks I have no redeeming social value.

The lists I make aren't your everyday normal-type lists. Take the lists I made in English on one boring gray day in February. We were supposed to be discussing an equally boring poem called "When You Are Old" by a guy named Yeats. The title alone is enough to put people to sleep. But apparently no one told Miss Brett that old isn't an interesting topic. Of course, nobody would dare. When Miss Brett came to town, it was on the back of a broom. So I started making a list.

Ten Things More Interesting than Discussing This Poem
1. Waiting for cells to mutate.

2. *Picking lint off wool slacks.*
3. *Watching streetlights change.*
4. *Buying dental floss—*

That's me in a nutshell for you. MARCUS T. JEN-KINS—THE KIND OF GUY WHO DEFINITELY BELIEVES DENTAL FLOSS IS MORE INTEREST-ING THAN POETRY! I also happen to think that professional basketball, Chinese food, Tarzan books, Mighty Mouse cartoons and Monty Python movies, girls, rock concerts, and the Summer Olympics all rate significantly higher in terms of interest than poetry. Unless, of course, the poetry has been written by Henry Yazzie.

"Who wants to read the first two stanzas of this poem for us?" Miss Brett asked. I didn't raise my hand because it's against my beliefs to participate in English class. In fact, I'm pretty sure all my hand-raising muscles have withered up and died by now.

Nobody else volunteered to read the poem either. They were probably bored like me—and a little afraid too. Miss Brett has that effect on people. My neighbor, Diana Rogers, finally raised her hand. Good old Diana. Teachers can always count on her to come through for them. Diana cleared her throat and began reading.

When you are old and gray and full of sleep,
And nodding by the fire, take down this book,
And slowly read, and dream of the soft look
Your eyes had once, and of their shadows deep;

How many loved your moments of glad grace,
And loved your beauty, with love false or true;
But one man loved the pilgrim soul in you,
And loved the sorrows of your changing face.

"Thank you, Diana," said Miss Brett with a smile that was supposed to be friendly. Miss Brett looked out at the class. "All right," she said. "What situation is the poet describing? What's going on in the poem?"

Although I don't like Miss Brett very much, I have to admit that she is an interesting person in a lot of ways. For one thing, she's beautiful. Not just pretty. But movie-star great-looking. Dark hair, fair skin, thick black brows, green eyes, a dynamite body for somebody her age, which I imagine is about thirty-five. She's smart too. But she's angry most of the time.

"Well?" Miss Brett demanded. Her eyes glittered, the way they always do when she gets irritated with us. She started prowling back and forth in front of the room like a big cat at the zoo.

"No comments?" Miss Brett asked. "Then let's look at this thing piece by piece, shall we? Is the speaker in the poem a man or a woman?"

"A man?" somebody guessed.

"And to whom is this man speaking?" Miss Brett asked.

"A woman?" someone else said.

I started another list: *Ten Reasons Why the Counselors Put Me in Honors English Even Though I Only Lower the Class Average.*

The Shadow Brothers

1. *I have a smart father (who's a shrink).*
2. *I have a smart foster brother (Henry, who is gifted).*
3. *I have a smart little sister (Julia, who was double-promoted to the sixth grade).*
4. *I have a smart neighbor (Diana).*
5. *They assume all this smartness must have rubbed off onto me—*

"The man and the woman in this poem," Miss Brett was saying, "—are they old or are they young?"

"Old?" someone guessed again.

"Oh, very good," Miss Brett said. "Perhaps that is why the poem is called 'When You Are Old.'"

The class laughed a little nervously.

"So what's this old man telling this old woman?"

No one answered. I looked at the clock on the wall, and then I saw Henry raise his hand.

Miss Brett's face softened a little. She likes Henry —which isn't too surprising, since Henry is basically brilliant in English. He wants to be a writer someday. He covers sports for the school newspaper, and then, of course, he does poetry.

There was a time I thought about being a writer too. When I was in grade school I read all of the Tarzan and Conan series, and I thought it would be really fun to do one of my own. I even created my own hero called the Master Marauder. Stupid idea, right?

"Henry, why don't you tell us what's going on in the poem?" Miss Brett said.

"The speaker is telling the woman that he loves

her, that he'll love her always, even after they've both grown old—"

I started another list: *Why Miss Brett Wants to See Henry After Class.*

When we'd walked into the classroom right before the bell, Miss Brett looked up and said, "Henry, I want to speak to you immediately after class." Her face said something was up. I felt nervous for him. Whatever it was, it was probably good—good things have a way of happening to Henry—but maybe it wasn't.

Henry had finished his explanation and Miss Brett started to say something more about the poem. Then she stopped. Right in the middle of her sentence.

"You know," she said, "I don't know why I even tried this poem out on you people. There's no way you can possibly appreciate what this means yet. People your age think nothing will ever change. In fact, you can't even conceive of a future with you in it beyond next weekend's date." She gave a short unfriendly laugh and snapped her book shut. "So let's try something different here. For tomorrow I want a poem modeled after this one—same meter, same structure. But I want you to call your poem 'When You Are Young'—"

I started another list. Remember that old Led Zeppelin song called "The Song Remains the Same"? They even made a movie out of it that shows sometimes as a midnight movie at Camelot Theater. My list was called *Things That Remain the Same.*

1. *Michael Jordan's unfailing genius with a hoop and basketball.*

2. *The greatness of the world's true literary
   masterpiece,* Tarzan and the Ant Men.
3. *Henry and me.*

Henry and Me. Me and Henry. It's been that way
forever. People even say our names together in the
same way they say Tom-and-Jerry. It's always Marcus-
and-Henry. Henry-and-Marcus.

I lucked out. How many people can say their
brother is also their best friend? Actually, Henry's my
foster brother, but that's just a technicality.

Miss Brett wrote out the assignment in strict detail
on the blackboard. One thing you have to say about
Miss Brett is that she's very clear about what she expects from students. I saw Diana, who is the most
conscientious person alive, copying the assignment
down into her notebook. Besides being conscientious
Diana is also one of these people who stick up for what
they believe in. Diana's big thing is animal rights. Last
year she got the only F of her life because she refused
to dissect a frog. This year she's organized the Wakara
High School Animal Rescue Team. Did I mention that
she's a vegetarian?

Diana is also one of the most original dressers I
know. She wears things like flight suits and baggy
khaki pants and huge sweatshirts. I think she buys
most of her clothes at the army-navy surplus store, and
her clothes are one of the many things that drive her
mother, DeeDee, crazy.

When the bell rang, everyone gathered up their
things and started to leave.

"Do you want me to wait?" I asked Henry.

"Yeah," he said, "if you don't mind."

Miss Brett went into her office at the front of the room. When everyone was gone, Henry picked up his books and stood by her office door.

"Come in, Henry." Miss Brett didn't shut the door behind them, so I could hear everything.

"I went ahead and did something without telling you about it first," she said. "I put together some of your best writing—mostly poems and essays as well as a few columns you've done for the school paper—and I sent them along with an application to *Teen Talk* magazine's summer youth internship program." There was a pause. "Guess what. They're interested in you. Really interested. There's a good chance they might select you as one of their summer interns and then you would get to spend the summer working for a magazine in New York City."

Even though I couldn't see his face, I knew he was too surprised to speak. Miss Brett went on. "They especially liked this poem of yours"—I heard a paper rustle—"about running at night. 'Star Runner.' "

Henry finally managed to say, "This is great. What am I supposed to do next?"

"They want to see more of your things and they want you to write a personal essay on this topic: 'The Me Nobody Knows.' This has to be done and sent back to New York by the end of April. Okay with you?"

"Okay. Thanks for taking the time to put all my stuff together like that. I mean it."

"Listen to me, Henry. You have a real gift. That means you also have a responsibility to develop it."

They walked out of her office, and Miss Brett practically jumped out of her skin when she saw me lurking outside her door. "I should have known you'd be waiting here, Marcus," she said with a smile that wasn't really a smile. *"Semper fidelis."*

Semper fidelis is the Marine motto and it means "always loyal." Fritz ordered patches that say SEMPER FI for us to sew on our velveteen theater jackets.

I don't think she meant it as a compliment.

"Whatever," I told her.

The classroom was starting to fill up with students. Miss Brett went to her desk and wrote out excuse slips. "So you two won't get in trouble for being late to your next class."

"Thanks," I said. Maybe Miss Brett didn't think I was such a clown after all. "Thanks," I said again.

But she'd already turned away to face the class.

Out in the hallway I gave Henry a high five. "All right," I said. "New York City!"

"Nothing's for sure yet," Henry said, but he was smiling too.

"Hey, I'll go with you. We'll see the Yankees at Yankee Stadium. We'll be there for the Mets at Shea. Diana will die of jealousy! I can hardly wait to tell her!" Diana loves baseball. She once won Henry's Cubs hat from him in our traditional New Year's Eve poker game. I don't think he's ever forgiven her.

"Hi, Henry."

Henry and I stopped dead in our tracks. Standing in front of us was Celia Cunningham and two of her friends—the School Fox flanked by a matched set of foxettes.

You know how there's always one girl in a school that all the guys love? Well, at Wakara High School it's Celia Cunningham. And here she was, standing in the hall being gorgeous and saying hello.

"Hi, Henry," she said again.

"Hi, Celia," said Henry.

She didn't seem to notice me. I stared at the ceiling and then at the floor and finally at my shoelaces. I've had lots of practice looking invisible like this, since I'm pretty standard-issue stuff—tall and thin with lots of straight reddish-brown hair, brown eyes, and freckles. Sometimes I look at myself in the mirror and say, "Hey, Marcus T. Jenkins! You look like a giraffe!"

Celia was wearing soft gray leather boots, blue jeans, and a fuzzy pink sweater. Her blond hair hung over her shoulders. She was looking mighty fine—better than fine, if you want to get specific about it.

Celia smiled and I thought I might go blind, her teeth were so white.

"Call me sometime, Henry," she said. Her voice was like a kiss, soft and a little breathy.

"Sure," said Henry. "That's a good idea. I will."

I wondered if he really would. Henry and I may think about girls a lot, but the truth is neither one of us has that much firsthand experience.

The bell rang.

"Uh-oh," said one of Celia's attendents. "We're late again."

"See you later, then," said Celia, smiling at Henry. I noticed her eyes were as blue as summer. I'd never seen more beautiful eyes in my whole life.

Celia and her friends walked past us on their way to class. Their perfume hung in the air behind them.

"Wow!" I said.

"Exactly," said Henry.

On our way to math I started making another list in my head. I've made this particular list before. *People I Would Much Rather Be Than Myself.* Usually the list looks something like this:

1. *Michael Jordan.*
2. *Magic Johnson.*
3. *Larry Bird.*

But today I varied the list a little. Today it looked like this:

1. *Henry Yazzie.*
2. *Henry Yazzie.*
3. *Henry Yazzie—*

First New York City. Now Celia Cunningham. I took a very deep breath and shoved my hands into my pockets.

3

HENRY YAZZIE. I can remember another time I wanted something that Henry Yazzie had.

When Henry first came to live with us, he didn't know how to ride a bike, even though he was seven years old. Not knowing how to ride a bike was just one of the things besides the color of his skin and the way he practically sang his words when he spoke that made Henry seem so different to me. There were times during the first few weeks he lived with us that I felt like I had a brand-new pal from Mars.

Henry came to live with us because my dad and Henry's father, Lennie, are old friends. There's a framed photograph of the two of them hanging on Dad's office wall. They're standing in front of a green short-bed pickup wearing plaid shirts and Stetsons. I always thought it was a pretty stupid picture of Dad. Whoever heard of a cowboy with glasses? Anyway, they met when Dad came out from Boston to spend a year working on the Navaho reservation where Lennie is a tribal police officer. Dad never went back East. He liked the West. He also liked my mother, a Utah

Mormon girl he met on a trip to Salt Lake City. Naturally, he decided to stick around and marry her.

Lennie Yazzie called my parents the summer before my second-grade year to ask if Henry could live with us and go to school with me. Lake View is a small but fairly affluent community between Salt Lake City and Provo. The schools have a good reputation, and Lennie said that's what Henry needed, since he was practically a genius. There were the government boarding schools, of course, but Lennie hated them. His own experience at one had made him self-conscious about being Navaho without really preparing him to make it in mainstream American society. Lennie wanted something different for his own son, so he decided to send Henry to Utah. Actually, this is not as unusual as it may seem. Over the years a number of Navahos have sent their kids to live with white families during the school year through the Mormon church's placement program.

There was one other thing. Henry's mother, Nora, had died earlier that spring. Lennie never said so, but Mom's always believed he was worried about raising Henry without her. Cops keep funny hours.

About a week after Lennie called, Dad and Mom came into my room one night to talk to me. I was playing cars on my bed, making caves and hills out of the wrinkled sheets. I had the world's greatest collection of Matchbox cars when I was seven years old.

"Marcus?"

I looked up. Dad sat down next to me, accidentally

mashing one of my volcanoes. Mom stood by the head of my bed and touched my hair.

"How would you like a Navaho Indian boy your own age to come live with us?" Dad asked me. "His name is Henry. He's the son of my friend, Lennie— the man in the picture at my office."

I wasn't really listening. "You're sitting on one of my trucks."

"He'd be your foster brother. That means he'd be a part of our family, even though he's not really related to us," Dad said.

"Okay." I made motor noises with my mouth.

"He'll have to share your room," Mom said.

I shrugged.

"We can put another twin bed right over there," Mom said to Dad.

"It might be a little tough for you at first, but I think you two could be very good friends, Marcus," said Dad. He kept looking at my face.

I looked back at him, wishing he would just get off my bed so I could find my truck.

Even though Mom and Dad checked out a zillion library books for me so I could learn about Navahos and even though they went to the reservation to meet Henry, the fact that I was going to have a new foster brother didn't seem real to me until he actually came.

Lennie was going to drive Henry to Lake View but got tied up on a case. Dad said to put him on a bus, and we'd be at the depot to pick him up. I remember thinking how lucky he was that he got to ride that bus all the way up from Arizona by himself.

"Henry, buddy!" Dad, who was juggling Julia on his hip, waved at him as he walked into the depot.

"Here we are, sweetheart!" Mom took my hand, then waved at Henry too.

Henry and I stared at each other. I noticed that he was a lot smaller than I was and that his eyes were big and black. He wasn't dressed like the Navaho kids I'd seen in the library books—he wasn't wearing beads or a headband. On the other hand he wasn't exactly dressed like me either. Henry had on a pair of shiny dress slacks and a white button-down shirt, while I was wearing shorts and a T-shirt that said MONSTER MANIA.

"Hi," I said.

Henry didn't say anything. Mom reached out and took one of his hands too.

When we got home Dad said, "Why don't you take Henry upstairs and show him your bedroom."

Henry followed me upstairs, still not saying a word.

"This is where you'll sleep," I said, pointing out the new twin bed. Then I took out all my stuff—G.I. Joes and Matchbox cars, my rock collection and a quart jar full of pennies—and showed everything to Henry. His eyes went wide, and I could tell he thought everything I had was really great. I *loved* showing it off.

"Hey, look!" I pointed. Our shadows flickered across the bedroom wall. "Stand behind me!" Henry did what I told him. The figures merged into one. Then we switched places, only I had to scrunch way down behind him to make my shadow fit.

"See?" I said. "Magic."

I was a big magic authority then.

I also took him to the room across the hall and showed him Julia, who was busy drooling and stuffing blankets into her mouth.

"This is my little sister," I said. "She can't talk yet."

Henry smiled at Julia and slipped his hand between the bars of her crib. She grabbed it, then started gnawing on it. Henry laughed and so did I. We looked at each other.

"Babies are kind of stupid," I explained.

But the thing Henry liked best was my bike—a red BMX with black racing stripes. Henry reached out to touch, then stroke it just like it was a cat.

"Here," I said pushing the bike toward him. "You can ride it."

Henry shook his head.

"Come on." I thought he was just being shy.

"I can't," he finally said in the soft little voice he used when he first came. "I don't know how."

It took me a minute to figure this out.

"You can't ride a bike?!" My mouth was probably hanging open down to my shins.

Henry tucked his head a little. "No."

"Do you want me to teach you how?"

He nodded. So that became the family project during the week before school started—teaching Henry how to ride my bike. Mom and Dad always let me demonstrate everything first, then Henry would climb on top and try to keep his balance. I can still remember the first time he rode it to the end of the sidewalk. He weaved and wobbled, but he didn't fall over.

"All right!" screamed my dad. "Let's hear it for Henry!" Henry and I gave each other five, which is something else I taught him how to do.

For a while there I thought having a foster brother was pretty cool. I used to wake up in the morning before he did and stare at him. I felt just like I was having a giant sleepover that never ended. I even bragged about him the first day at school the way some kids might brag about getting a new dog or a Nintendo machine. "Hey, guys," I told everybody, "this is our new Navaho brother." I couldn't help but notice that he was the only one in the entire class with brown skin.

But then the newness wore off and sometimes there were things I didn't like about having someone new come to stay with us, even though I liked Henry himself. I got tired of sharing *my* bedroom, and I for sure didn't want him to play with my stuff unless I said he could first. Sometimes I got tired of him following me around, and I even wished he'd go away.

But the worst was when Dad came home the day after Thanksgiving with a present for Henry.

"Henry," Dad called when he got home from work. "You and Marcus turn off the TV and come here."

He had a big grin on his face when he walked into the family room. "Let's go outside. I've got something to show you guys."

Henry looked at me, and I raised my shoulders to show him I didn't know what was going on.

"Hurry up," said Dad.

We followed him outside, and there it was sitting in the driveway—a brand new green Sting-Ray bicycle with a fake gearbox.

It was the gearbox that got to me. I didn't have one on my bike.

"It's for you, Henry, from all of us," Dad said. "Now you and Marcus can ride bikes together."

Henry stared at it like he'd never seen a bicycle before, and then a look of understanding went on in his eyes. He faced Dad, with a little growing smile.

"Take her for a spin," said Dad. Henry grabbed the bike suddenly, like somebody might try to take it away from him. He lifted the kickstand with his heel, climbed on, and took off down the street.

My heart was banging inside my chest and my face felt hot. My stomach was doing triple flips. Suddenly I exploded.

"No fair!" I screamed at my dad.

Dad looked at me, blinking in surprise.

"It's *no fair!*" I said it even louder this time as my eyes started to blur.

"But, buddy," Dad said reasonably, "I thought you'd be happy for Henry to have his own bike. Now you won't have to share yours."

"*His* bike has gears!"

"Well, they aren't *real* gears," Dad said, sounding a little exasperated. His glasses were slipping down his nose like crazy and he kept pushing them back into place. "I just had the guy at the bike shop attach a fake gearbox." This is the fatal mistake adults—even trained professionals like my dad—sometimes make with little kids. They miss the real point.

I stood in the middle of the driveway, shaking. "I hate you!" Then I ran straight into the house.

Later that evening I found Henry in our room, playing with some of my cars. I stomped over to him and ripped a dump truck out of his hands. "Don't touch my stuff ever again!" I yelled at him. At first Henry looked startled. And then he did something I'd never seen him do before.

He started to cry.

Only, he didn't cry like I did. He didn't make any noise. He didn't sob or shake or make choking noises in the back of his throat. He just sat completely still there on the floor while the tears slid down his cheeks.

I would have been much happier if he had hit me or at least called me a snothead, which is what I called Julia when Mom wasn't listening.

"Don't cry. I'm sorry." I was, too. I even gave him back the truck, but nothing stopped his quiet tears.

That was the night Henry got sick. At first Mom thought it was just a twenty-four-hour flu bug, but he didn't get better. I went back to school on Monday without him and Tuesday and Wednesday too. He was still sick at the end of the week. One night Dad walked out of our room into the hall where I was standing with Mom.

"He keeps calling for his grandfather," he told us,

frowning a little. "He wants his grandfather to get a *hataali*."

"What?" Mom asked.

"Hataali. I think it means medicine man."

Fear spread throughout my whole body, making my hands and feet go cold. I'd yelled at Henry for playing with my stuff and now he was sick. Maybe he was going to die, and if he did it would be my fault. I was too scared to talk.

My parents called Henry's dad that night and everybody decided that maybe Henry should go back to the reservation for a while. Dad, Henry, and I left for northern Arizona a few days before Christmas vacation.

The farther south we drove, the stranger things started to look to me. I'd never been to southern Utah before, and I was surprised to see the land flatten out and turn real red. The orange mountains and hills jumped out of nowhere—like islands in a desert ocean. They were strange shapes too. One hill looked like a saltshaker. Another looked like an upside-down sombrero. Still another looked like organ pipes. There were scrubby junipers and piñon pines, twisted by years of heat and wind. A few dead trees were poised against the open sky, just like snakes ready to strike. A light snow glazed everything. Sometimes fog swirled up in front of us like ghosts.

Henry sat by a window and fiddled with the automatic lock—up and down, up and down, up and down. Usually it drove Dad crazy whenever Henry or I played with the locks, but this time he didn't say anything. The closer we got to the reservation, the more Henry started to bounce around in the car. Dad didn't even make him keep his seat belt on.

"Hey, look at that!" Dad pointed out the window at a large brown animal on the side of the road picking at something that was dead.

"Is it a coyote?" I asked. I knew that coyotes lived in the desert and that they howled at the moon every night.

Henry laughed. "Eagle."

"It's a golden eagle," said Dad. "They're quite rare. Even here. Look at him, Marcus! Isn't he terrific?"

The bird turned fierce eyes on us and took flight the instant we passed it. I was so startled that I screamed right out loud, which made me feel completely stupid. Dad put his hand on the back of my neck and gave me a little squeeze.

We took Henry to the trailer where his father lives. Dad practically cracked his skull as he was crawling out of the car.

"Ouch!"

There was a friendly laugh. "Hey, now, *that's* using your head." It was Lennie, stepping out of the trailer to greet us. He wore boots, Levi's, a plaid shirt, and a Stetson—just like his picture in Dad's office.

"Ya-tah-hey," Dad greeted him.

Lennie nodded and adjusted his hat. Then he scooped Henry up in his arms and growled like a bear, which made Henry squeal with laughter. When he put

Henry down, he fished in his shirt pocket and pulled out a sucker.

"This is for you." He handed it to me and smiled. Henry hugged Lennie around the legs.

"Well, good-bye, Henry," Dad said when we got ready to leave. He put his arms around him and kissed his hair. "We sure love you, buddy."

Henry looked straight at me with big black eyes.

As we were leaving the reservation we stopped off at a trading post and I saw an old Navaho woman wearing a heavy blue velvet shirt, a long skirt, and a pair of old running shoes. She had a couple of little kids with her, and they kept staring at *me* like I was the strangest thing they'd ever seen. I looked around the store, and I realized that my dad and I were the only white people there, just like Henry had been the only brown person in our class the first day of school. Now I was the one from Mars.

On the way home again I felt the same fear I'd felt when Henry was sick, the fear that somehow everything that had happened was my fault.

"Will Henry come back to us?" I asked Dad.

"I don't know. He's awful homesick, Marcus."

We didn't say anything for a minute. There was nothing but the hum of tires.

"I love you, Daddy."

Dad put his arm around my shoulder and pulled me close to him. But I still felt afraid.

At home everything felt pretty empty without Henry around. I missed watching cartoons with him in the morning and sometimes I was scared at night now that I was all alone in my room.

We called Henry on Christmas Day. My stomach hurt the whole time I talked to him.

"What's the matter, honey?" Mom asked when I got off the phone. I guess she could tell something was wrong just by looking at my face.

I had to tell someone so I whispered it in her ear. "I think Henry went away because of me."

She looked at me. "Why do you think that?"

I didn't know how to tell her about the dump truck I took away from him. I didn't know how to tell her that sometimes I used to wish he'd go away.

Mom pulled me close to her. "Henry didn't go away because of you. Don't ever think that." I buried my face in her sweater so deep, I could smell her perfume. I liked having her hold me. But I didn't believe her.

That's why when Henry came back to us after Christmas vacation I felt like everything had been made right again. You know how goofy kids get about things? Well, I thought this was God's little way of telling me that everything was okay, that I'd been forgiven.

We were best friends after that. We were brothers. And when spring came we started dragging our sleeping bags outside—just the two of us—to look at the stars. Sometimes we got mad at each other, but he was never mean to me.

And I made sure I was never mean to him.

Henry brought two red rocks from the reservation

—one for him, one for me. I used to look at mine, turning it over and over in my hands. It was the best thing in my rock collection. No doubt about it. Still, in my heart I was glad my family had saved Henry from a place where coyotes suddenly turned into birds and trees into snakes.

And the colors were so bright that they hurt your eyes.

4

WE SAW CELIA AGAIN at lunch the day after she spoke to Henry in the hall.

Diana, Henry, and I were eating together as usual. Henry and Diana were continuing an argument about sex roles—are men and women the way they are because society makes them that way or are they just born that way?—that they had started earlier in Current Events. Arguing is Henry and Diana's favorite mode of communication. Only, they have completely different debating styles. Diana gets very emotional. Her voice gets louder and her face gets red. Henry, on the other hand, stays cool. He stays cool in everything he does.

I was busy playing with my Jell-O salad.

"Do you guys ever wonder why Jell-O wiggles?" I asked. "Like what makes it do *that*?" I poked the Jell-O salad with my fork and watched it shiver.

Henry and Diana stopped arguing and stared at me.

"*What?*" Diana said. "What are you babbling about, Marcus?"

I didn't answer her. I don't know about you, but it sort of takes it out of me when a girl tells me I babble. Even if the girl is only Diana.

"Henry?" It was another girl's voice. Henry and I turned around.

Celia smiled and I wondered what she was doing here in the lunchroom holding two cans of Diet Pepsi in her hands instead of posing for magazine covers somewhere.

"Hi," she said, and I noticed again what a great-sounding voice she has.

"Hi," said Henry.

Henry and Celia looked at one another.

"I put two quarters in the drink machine over there and look what I got." Celia held up the two cans of Diet Pepsi. "Two for the price of one."

Henry laughed, and Celia did too.

"Anyway, I thought I'd give the extra one to you." Celia smiled again. She handed the can to Henry and their fingers touched. Henry wasn't in any big hurry to take the can away from her.

Celia opened her own drink and took a long sip, then licked the foam away with her tongue. "I was wondering why you didn't call me last night." She didn't sound angry or hurt. Just a little amused.

I could tell Henry didn't know what to say.

"He was working last night," I said, like I was giving testimony to the police. "He can even prove it." Celia looked at me briefly, then locked her eyes on Henry again.

"No big deal," she said. Her eyelids flickered shut

for a minute, and I noticed how long her eyelashes were. "I'd just really like for you to call me sometime."

"I will," Henry said. "I promise."

"Good!" Celia gave a light laugh. "Well, I have to go to art class now. I'm finishing up a project for my portfolio. I'll see you later, then." She nodded at me and Diana both, after smiling one last time at Henry. We watched her walk away.

"And the earth moved," I said, quoting the only line I remembered from Hemingway.

Diana was frowning.

"I don't like her," she said.

Henry looked at Diana the way Dad looks at Julia when she deserves a slow and unpleasant death.

"Hey, what's not to like?" I asked.

"I think—I think she's insincere."

Henry snorted. "Do you have something specific to base your observation on? Has Celia been saying particularly insincere things to you lately?"

Diana glared at Henry. "Girls like Celia Cunningham don't bother to say anything at all to girls like me." She picked up a breadstick. *Snap!* She broke the breadstick in two, then jammed a piece of it into her bowl.

"Well, would you even give her a chance to say something to you?" Henry asked.

"Now, what's that suppose to mean?" Diana demanded.

"Admit it. Don't you think it's true that girls sometimes jump to false conclusions about someone who looks like Celia because they feel threatened?" Henry was smiling a little because he knew he probably had Diana there. "I happen to think that's pretty *sexist*. Don't you?"

He emphasized the word *sexist* because Diana uses it all the time.

"All right!" I yelled, like I was a spectator at a basketball game. Henry and I gave each other five.

Diana swore loudly at both of us as her cheeks turned pink.

"Aw, come on, Diana," I said. "Don't be a poor loser."

Diana picked up her tray and moved to another table.

"DIANA WAS PRETTY STEAMED at lunch today," Henry said as we were slipping on our sweats before track practice.

"Yeah," I agreed. "She certainly was."

He stooped over to tie one of his shoelaces. "She takes things too seriously." Henry likes to argue with Diana, but it bothers him when things get out of hand. She'd never gotten up and walked away from him before.

"She might be a little touchy about the subject of Celia," I said slowly.

Henry looked up from his shoes. "*Why?* They don't even know each other."

"Well, it's not too hard to see that DeeDee would love to have somebody like Celia Cunningham for a daughter," I told him. DeeDee is Diana's very rich and very good-looking mother.

The Shadow Brothers

Henry and I get along great with DeeDee. She always brings us things home from her trips around the world—wineskins from Spain, kangaroo pelts from Australia, and (I'm not making this up) grass skirts and coconut bras from Hawaii. DeeDee is pretty outrageous. Once she gave us the keys to her car before we even had our driver's licenses and told us to steal all the neighbors' lawn chairs and store them in her garage just for the heck of it. When she's feeling good, DeeDee sits on our porch and tells us extremely funny stories about her wild days at the University of Utah where she majored in a) shopping and b) partying. She's the only adult I know who talks to us straight—I can't imagine my own mother telling me stories about getting bombed, for example. I *like* the way DeeDee talks to us, frankly.

Her main problem is that she keeps getting married. She's been married three times now and each guy she marries makes more money than the last guy did. But pretty soon DeeDee starts to drink too much again and before long the new husband checks out.

DeeDee and Diana don't get along. I actually think Diana confuses DeeDee. What she wanted was a very pretty daughter who enjoys clothes and parties as much as she does. What she got instead was a great big lumberjack of a girl with flaming red hair who wears fatigues to school and spends her weekends doing extra-credit homework.

"Diana isn't bad looking," said Henry. "She's got nice legs."

"But she's no Celia Cunningham," I pointed out

quickly. Discussing the finer points of Diana's anatomy made me uncomfortable.

Henry bent over and started lacing up his other shoe.

Mike Donahue, the track coach, walked up.

"I need to talk to you guys," he said. "Finish changing, then come see me in my office." I couldn't read a thing from his face.

When we knocked on Donahue's door, my palms were sweating. What if Donahue was going to cut me from the team? But then why did he want to see Henry too? I took a deep breath.

"Come on in." Donahue was standing by a window in the rear of his office, looking out onto the field.

I noticed how gray Donahue's sideburns were getting, but he still looked like a runner—lean and strong. In his day Donahue was one of the greats. He ran with Jim Ryun at the University of Kansas. That's behind him, but now he's a great coach. They don't come any better.

"I got a problem here," he said, still looking out the window, "and I need you to help me out." Then he turned around and stared at Henry and me with those metal-gray eyes of his that made you think he could see kryptonite through a lead box if he wanted to.

"What's going on, Coach?" Henry asked.

"Come over here and take a look out this window." Donahue pointed to a kid who was standing by himself on the field. He had long thick black hair that hung straight to his shoulders. His skin was a dark burned brown. He bent over, legs crossed, and put his palms flat on the ground.

I caught my breath. The kid was Indian. *Native American,* as my parents would say.

"Say hello to one great big headache," said Donahue. He walked to his desk and sat down. Henry and I took the chairs in front of his desk. Without knowing exactly why, I felt even more nervous and I wiped my hands on the knees of my sweats.

What did Henry think? All during junior high school and now for the past two years at Wakara High, he'd been the only Indian. His face was as closed as a closed book.

"His name's Frank," Donahue said. "He was over at Scenic View High until last week. The only Native American kid there this year. But he had trouble. Lots of it. He walked through the door and bad things started happening. The counselors there thought he might do a little better here." Donahue looked straight at Henry.

Something passed over Henry's face and then it was gone.

"Why?" asked Henry. "Because I'm an *Indian* too?" Something made his voice sound different. Resentment, maybe?

Donahue nodded. "That's exactly what they thought."

He leaned back in his chair, lifted his feet up onto his desk, and let out a long sigh. "The kid's been on the reservation up until this past year. Then his mother converted to the Mormon church and decided it would be good for Frank to come up here to live with a nice big Mormon family. She wants him to convert too." Donahue snorted. "I'd say the chances of that happening are pretty much slim to none."

"He's not happy here?" Henry asked, more of a statement than a question.

"You got it," said Donahue. "Can't say that I blame the poor kid. It must be hard having to get used to a new school and a new family *and* a new culture all at once. Of course, I guess you know something about that yourself, Yazzie." Donahue lifted his feet off the desk, leaned forward in his chair, and looked directly at Henry.

"I don't know. I don't remember much. I was only seven at the time," Henry said in a completely flat voice.

Donahue shrugged and reached into his pocket for a pack of Juicy Fruit gum. He offered Henry and me a stick. "I wouldn't think you'd forget a thing like that."

You could tell Donahue didn't buy what Henry had said for a minute. He put a piece of gum in his mouth and chewed it for a while. Nobody said a word. I shifted my weight and Donahue looked at me.

"What about it, Jenkins? Can you remember what it was like for Yazzie here when he first came? He must have felt"—Donahue searched for the right word—"different. Were there things your family did that he didn't understand?"

"I don't remember anything either," I mumbled quickly. I didn't want Donahue looking through me the way he'd just looked through Henry.

Donahue got up and went to the window again. He folded his arms across his chest and spoke without looking at us.

"I'm not trying to pry into your personal business. I just want you both to remember how things must have been, because I'm going to ask you to do me one big unpleasant favor."

Donahue turned around. "I need you to help me out with Frank. Be his pal. Show him the ropes. Do whatever you can to make his life a little easier here. Can you guys do that for me?"

I nodded and so did Henry. I think Henry would do just about anything for Donahue. My dad always says that Henry may have been born with wings on his heels, but it was Mike Donahue who showed him how to use them. Henry nearly tied the state record for the mile run last year, and he was just a sophomore. Like I say. Gifted. All the way around.

"By the way," said Donahue casually as Henry and I were getting ready to leave. "I think you ought to know that Frank can run."

I thought it was about time for me to make an intelligent contribution to the conversation. "Yeah?" I said.

"Yeah," said Donahue. "I called his old high school in New Mexico. The PE teacher there said that Frank was the best long-distance runner he'd ever seen, and he wondered what the hell he was doing up here where he doesn't belong."

He opened his door. "Get out of here, you guys. Take Frank on a run."

Henry and I went outside. The ground was still covered with snow, and the wind bit through my sweats. I could hardly wait to start running. It's not that I love workouts, but I knew that running would warm me up.

"Where is he?" asked Henry. "Where'd the guy go? He was here just a few minutes ago."

I looked around. I didn't see a sign of him either. Frank was gone.

I saw Henry shiver.

Frank had disappeared. Just like a ghost.

5

HENRY AND I WERE ALL PREPARED to help Frank out, but Frank didn't do his part. He didn't show for practice again for the rest of the week, and he didn't show for his classes either. It's kind of tough to be friends with someone who isn't there in either body or spirit.

On Friday Donahue talked to us in his office.

"I don't know what to do about that kid. The counselors told me he wanted to run, but he sure doesn't act like it."

We were all quiet for a minute, then Henry said, "It's sort of hard to say, but . . . some Native Americans have a different sense of time than we do"— Henry looked embarrassed—"than *Anglos* do."

"I don't understand," said Donahue.

"Schedules, dates, deadlines, appointments—I don't think it's as important to some of them to meet those things as it is to Anglos." Henry shrugged. "I can't explain it any better than that. They don't feel *controlled* by time. That's true of some Navahos, anyway."

"So Frank may be missing practice because he lost track of time?" asked Donahue.

"Maybe he just got busy doing something else that seemed more important to him at the moment."

"Okay, then," said Donahue, "we'll just play it by ear for a while."

All during practice I thought about what Henry had said. To tell you the truth, his comment surprised me a little. He fits in so well here that I hardly even notice he's Navaho anymore. The only time I do is when Lennie stays with our family.

Henry doesn't go back to the reservation much now because he's too busy—school in the winter, baseball in the summer. So Lennie comes up here a couple of times every year instead. I like Lennie. He's a very funny guy with a million great stories about being a reservation cop. It's not hard to see where Henry gets his sense of humor.

Still, they don't seem very much alike to me. You look at Lennie sitting there in his plaid cotton shirt with mother-of-pearl buttons, talking about rounding up sheep thieves, and you realize that he lives in a completely different world than Henry.

And then there was the time Lennie discovered that Henry was driving a hearse around town.

"Whoever heard of a Navaho owning a hearse?" he asked, shaking his head.

Navahos, Dad explained later, traditionally avoid anything connected with death.

So, if you ask me, Henry is more Jenkins than Yazzie.

I gave him a bad time about our conversation with Donahue after practice. "Since when did you become the big expert on Indian affairs?" I was driving him to the theater. He had the six-to-eleven shift.

Henry smiled, then lifted a foot and put it on the dashboard. "Well, I *am* Navaho, in case you never noticed."

I squinted at him, then opened my eyes wide with surprise. I slapped my own face. "Why, so you are!"

Henry laughed, then looked out the window. "I haven't forgotten *everything*, Marcus."

I rolled the hearse up onto the sidewalk in front of the theater and made two girls with identical blond hairdos jump straight off the ground and scream out loud at the same time. It was great.

This really broke Henry up. "Fritz hates it when you do that," he said, laughing. Then he smiled and waved at the girls, who were busy checking the damage to their hairdos. Both of them flipped us off, which made Henry laugh even more.

"Some people," I said, "have no sense of humor at all."

TALK ABOUT WEIRD COINCIDENCES. There was a letter from Lennie sitting in the mailbox when I got home. It was addressed in neat capital letters to Henry Yazzie. I tucked the mail underneath my arm.

"Mom?" I yelled through the house.

"In here, Marcus!"

I found her sitting at the kitchen table, surrounded by stacks of books and papers. Mom is going back to school, because she wants to become a social worker and save the world. As if one shrink for a parent wasn't enough.

Since Mom has gone back to school, she's grown out her hair and had it permed. She's also started to wear oversized sweaters and big round red glasses instead of contacts because she thinks the glasses make her look smarter. I always tell her that she's having a midlife crisis, but the truth is that I'm pretty proud of her. I think it takes a lot of guts for someone her age to go back to school.

"We need to talk," she said.

I moved the morning newspaper and one of Julia's ballet slippers from a chair so I could sit down. Since Mom has gone back to school, the house has fallen apart. Henry's the only person who ever picks things up. Dad, Julia, and I—we're all gifted slobs.

"Your English teacher called me this afternoon."

"What did Attila the Hen want?" I'd once heard Margaret Thatcher, the prime minister of Great Britain, called that. It seemed like an appropriate name for Miss Brett too.

Mom ignored my crack. "She said she can't continue to carry you in Honors English if you don't do the work."

I didn't say anything.

"We've been through this before, honey. I thought after last semester you wouldn't let this happen again."

I started drumming my fingers on the kitchen table.

"Stop that. Do you *want* to be dropped from Miss Brett's class?"

"That would be fine. Great. Wonderful. I never wanted to take Honors in the first place. I told you and Dad that, but you wouldn't listen."

Mom peered at me thoughtfully through her glasses. "That's true. We just wanted you to be challenged. You used to be a very good English student."

I shrugged.

"And you used to love to write. Remember those cute little stories you used to make up about that big green man with the silver horns and hairy toes?"

"The Master Marauder," I said. "Those stories weren't supposed to be cute."

She laughed, and I had to smile. It's hard for me to stay mad around Mom for very long.

"So what are you going to do about this situation?" Mom asked.

In the old days, before she decided to become Mother Teresa, Mom would have just told me to shape up or else. Now she has a new technique—trying to get me to accept responsibility for my own life. What a drag.

"I'll hand in my work."

Mom pulled a face at me. "Once more, with feeling."

"I do hereby solemnly swear to hand in my work."

"Including the upcoming essay on *Moby Dick.*"

I groaned.

"Marcus—"

"Including the upcoming essay on *Moby Dick*." Anything to get her off my back.

"*Good* work, too, Marcus. Okay?" I nodded, and she grinned. "Now, that part wasn't so hard, was it?" She leaned back in her chair and stretched. "How about a Coke?"

Mom craves caffeine with every fiber in her body. My autobiography will be called *My Mother Is a Caffeine Addict.* I got up and found two Cokes in the fridge. I opened one for her. I drank my Coke slowly, rolling it around in my mouth before swallowing.

"Henry got a letter from Lennie today," I said.

"Oh, good!" said Mom, taking a sip. "It's been a while since we've heard from him." She frowned a little. "Speaking of Henry, I want to ask you about the possibility—now, don't get mad at me—that you're doing poorly in English because it's Henry's best subject? I'm wondering if you're afraid to compete with him."

"Thanks for your analysis, Mrs. Freud," I said, practically choking on my drink. I was getting mad again.

"You've always been a good friend to Henry. Right from the very first day. But that doesn't mean you have to play second fiddle to him. Nobody expects you to do that. Especially not Henry. There's no reason why you can't do as well as he does."

I snorted with disgust and looked out the kitchen window. It was dark already.

I'm not afraid of competing with Henry, I wanted to tell her. *You couldn't be more wrong.*

But a cold fire burned beneath my ribs when I thought about her words.

AT TEN-FIFTY THE TELEPHONE RANG. I grabbed it. Maybe Fritz had done something totally uncharacteristic and let Henry off early.

"Marcus! This is Diana." She was whispering.

"Speak up."

"I don't want my mother to hear me," Diana said. "I really need your help."

I knew what was coming.

"I just got a call from somebody who said they thought they heard a cat meowing in the Dumpster behind the bowling alley downtown. I need you to take me there."

"A rescue, Diana? It's nearly midnight." But I should have known that wouldn't matter. Not to the Clara Barton of the cat world.

"Please," she said.

I sighed. "Okay. I have to pick Henry up first, though. It's on the way."

"He better be waiting," she said, and hung up.

Diana met me at the hearse with a blanket stuffed under her arm. She was wearing duck shoes, a baggy jacket, a long knit scarf, and Henry's old Cubs baseball cap. It occurred to me right then that Diana dresses the way she does to hide herself. She hates the fact that she's tall, and I guess she figures if she buries herself under layers of clothes no one will notice. But her clothes only draw attention to her size, which I'm sure DeeDee has told her a million times.

"I hope Boston doesn't whine too much while I'm gone," she said. "I don't want him to wake up my mother. Let's hurry, Marcus."

We got in the hearse and headed downtown. I flipped on the radio and caught the end of "Stairway to Heaven." It was beginning to snow.

"Lovely weather," I said to no one in particular. The hearse answered me with the slap of the windshield wipers.

Henry was waiting for us. He was a little surprised to see Diana.

"A rescue," I explained.

Henry rolled his eyes.

We drove toward the bowling alley.

"Do you want to know why Fritz doesn't have any girls working at the theater?" Henry asked. "He told me tonight."

You know how it is in most theaters—girls sell tickets and popcorn, boys take tickets and usher. Not at Camelot Theater. No, sir. Camelot is manned by men.

"This ought to be interesting," I said.

"He doesn't like having women work for him because they crack under pressure. They're not combat hardy."

I swore out loud, then laughed. "Somebody needs to explain to Fritz that he's running a theater, not a platoon."

"Do you think Fritz is right, Diana? Do women crack under pressure?" Henry was working very hard to start an argument with Diana. But Diana wasn't biting. She had other things on her mind.

"There's the bowling alley! The Dumpster's in the back."

As I parked the hearse, Diana whipped a flashlight out of her jacket like she was Dirty Harry pulling a .44 Magnum from his holster. She was out of the hearse before we'd even come to a complete stop, stalking toward the Dumpster.

"Ever notice how Diana moves?" Henry asked. "She doesn't just walk. She strides. She lopes. She bursts through doorways."

"You make her sound like a one-woman SWAT team."

Henry laughed.

By now she was trying to lift the lid on the Dumpster.

"Come on. Let's help her—if she'll let us," Henry said.

The three of us lifted the lid together. We heard a very faint meow. Diana began talking in a low, calm voice.

"Hang on, baby. We're coming for you." She handed the flashlight to Henry and told me to hold the lid up.

"Shine the light where I tell you to," she said, and hiked a long leg over the side of the Dumpster. She boosted herself in.

DeeDee would just love this.

Diana began sifting through the garbage piece by piece. Even though it was cold, the smell of spoiling food filled my nose. I thought I might throw up.

Another faint meow. How long had the cat been in there? It sounded pretty far gone.

"Over here, Henry." Diana pointed. "Shine the light over here."

She waded through the garbage toward the light. She reached into the garbage and pulled out a bag.

"Ah-ha!" she said. The bag squirmed and then it went limp. "Hurry! In the hearse!"

I tried to help her out of the Dumpster, but she slapped me away. She handed the bag to Henry and crawled out.

"You really smell lovely," I said.

The three of us climbed into the hearse. Diana placed the bag on the car seat, untied it, and reached in carefully.

"Ouch!" she yelped, then smiled. "You've got a little spit left in you, huh? Well, that's good. That's really good." She pulled the cat out. It wasn't full grown, but it wasn't exactly a kitten either. It was brindle colored, and the most interesting thing about it was its face. Half of it was black, the other half was orange. It looked like someone had taken a paintbrush and drawn a line straight down the middle of its nose. The cat also looked very hungry.

Diana grabbed her blanket and wrapped it around the cat, then placed it on the seat beside her. "Let's go."

As we drove home, I kept looking at the cat, wondering who would do something like that—wrapping it up in a bag and leaving it to die.

"Makes you sick, doesn't it?" Diana practically read my mind.

"Yeah, it does," said Henry. The cat looked straight at him and meowed.

"Oh, no!" Diana laughed. "He likes you, Henry."

"Oh, right," he said. But he was smiling.

"Cats choose their people. Maybe he's choosing you."

Henry laughed.

"I'm serious, Henry. Actually, I think you have the makings of a true cat person, Henry Yazzie. Cats are cool, aloof, intelligent. They're neatness freaks too. Just like you."

Henry reached for the cat and began stroking its head. At first it flinched. But after a while it relaxed. And even though the cat was practically dead, it did the most amazing thing. It started to purr.

The purring probably did it. Once it started purring, Henry decided to keep it. He called it Lazarus because he'd brought it back from the dead. Henry picked up the cat and cradled it against his chest. Lazarus closed his eyes.

"You're going inside with me," Henry told the cat. Then he turned to Diana.

"Sometimes you're okay." And then he smiled.

6

BETWEEN WORK and running a rescue with Diana, Henry didn't see the letter from his father until the next morning.

"This came for you yesterday, Henry." Mom handed the letter to him at the breakfast table.

Henry took it and looked at it for a minute. Then he put it in his jeans pocket without opening it. "I'll read it on the way to school. Thanks."

I took a last gulp of my orange juice. "Time to go!" Henry and I got up to leave.

"Don't forget Julia," Mom called after us. "You promised to give her a ride."

Julia emerged from her bedroom as if on cue and stood at the top of the stairs like Miss America.

"Hey, move it, Legs!"

She smiled a phony smile and waved a phony wave while walking slowly down the steps. She does this whenever she wants to drive me crazy.

"Don't call me Legs," she said when she finally got to the bottom. "I told you before that I don't like it."

One thing about Julia—she knows exactly what she

likes and doesn't like, which is more than I can say about myself sometimes.

We picked up Diana. She and Julia sat in the back. Henry and I sat in the front. He took his father's letter out of his pocket and opened it very carefully.

He swore when he was finished reading it.

"Hen-ry," said Julia in her schoolteacher voice. "No swear-ing!"

"What's the matter?" I asked.

"Nothing." He refolded the letter and slipped it back into the envelope. This is just one of the differences between Henry and me. Henry has an envelope to put letters back into. By the time I get the letter out, I've usually mangled the envelope.

The hearse was quiet. Diana was reading and Henry wasn't talking, so I flipped on the radio.

"It's my dad," Henry said finally. "He's writing for my grandfather."

"Why didn't your grandpa write you himself?" Julia asked.

"He doesn't know how," said Henry. "He can't read either. My grandfather is very traditional. He lives in a hogan. He believes in ghosts."

I don't know why, but for a split second I thought of Frank, the way he'd been there one minute and gone the next. Then I thought about what Henry had just said. I could hardly believe my ears. This is a) the twentieth century and b) America. You figure everyone reads—even if it's only the back of a cereal box first thing in the morning. You also figure people don't believe in ghosts.

"He wants me to come home for the summer."

I practically slammed on the brakes. "Get serious."

"My grandfather is getting old and wants to teach me things before he dies. Customs, traditions, rituals —the Navaho Way. My grandfather never did like the idea of my going away. He thought I should have stayed with my mother's people. Obviously my dad disagreed."

"Well, you *can't* go back this summer," I said. "You're going to be in New York City."

"Come on, Marcus. New York is a long shot." Henry shifted in his seat. "I haven't even started writing my essay yet about the me nobody knows."

For some reason I found myself getting very angry with Henry's father. He hardly wrote anymore. As far as I was concerned, he barely existed. Now suddenly he was showing up in Henry's life, making demands.

And for some funny reason I started feeling pretty irritated with Henry too. He should have just laughed and made some sort of joke when he read the letter, he should have crumpled it up into a little ball. He should have stuffed it into an ashtray, just to show how stupid the idea of returning to the reservation was.

Diana closed the book she'd been reading. I could tell she was interested in our conversation.

"I think you ought to consider going home for a while, Henry," she said.

"*What?* Are you nuts?"

Diana looked at me like I was the crazy one. "His grandfather would obviously like to spend some time with him before he dies. I'm just saying that ought to count for something." Diana was using her reasonable voice. I like it better when she's hysterical because it's easier to ignore what she's saying.

"Maybe," I said, "but Henry's got a life of his own. He's busy. He's got plans. Sometimes a person has to put himself first."

Diana snorted. "This world would be a much better place if we all put other people first every now and then. After all, we are talking about Henry's family here."

No we're not, I thought. *That's not what we're talking about at all. Henry may share a name with Lennie and his grandfather, but Dad, Mom, Julia, and me— we're his real family.*

"Will you two please stop talking about me like I'm not even here?" Henry said. "Don't worry about me. I'll take care of things."

I glared at Diana. She glared back. I had the funny feeling that Henry and I had suddenly switched places. Now *I* was the guy arguing with Diana and he was the guy just staring out the window. Nobody said anything the rest of the way to school.

As we were walking up the stairs to the front door of the school, somebody called, "Henry."

Diana kept right on going, but Henry and I turned around. Celia started walking toward Henry.

"Oh," he said. "Hi, Celia."

"I keep waiting for you to call," she said. "You promised." She looked over Henry's shoulder straight at me.

Never let it be said that Marcus T. Jenkins doesn't

know how to take a hint. I left the two of them standing alone on the stairs with the morning sun shining on Celia's hair.

I WAS BEGINNING TO THINK that Frank must have been kidnapped by aliens and dropped from a high altitude over Nevada somewhere, but he surprised us all by showing up to practice.

Henry and I saw him stretching out on the field.

"Come on," said Henry. "Let's go talk to him."

We trotted over.

"Hi," said Henry.

"Yo," I said. I said "yo" even though I realize the only people who say "yo" are a) nerds and b) people in Sylvester Stallone movies.

Frank turned around. His eyes opened with surprise when he first saw Henry, then narrowed again. He didn't say anything—he just kept stretching out.

"Okay if we join you?" Henry asked.

Frank shrugged.

The three of us stretched out for a while until Frank stood up.

"Ready to go?" Henry asked.

Frank shrugged again. I was beginning to decide that verbal must not be Frank's style. He fell into a loose, easy stride, and Henry and I joined him. It was cold enough outside that I could see my breath every time I exhaled.

"Look," said Henry as we jogged around the track and through the gate onto the street, "my name is Henry Yazzie."

"Navaho," said Frank. Only, he didn't just say it. He practically spit the word right out of his mouth.

"Yeah. That's right," said Henry. He was just as surprised by Frank's reaction as I was.

Frank didn't say anything more, but I noticed he was picking up the pace. Henry matched him stride for stride, and so did I.

"I figure we ought to run around five miles this afternoon," said Henry.

"You run five," said Frank. "I'll run ten."

Ten miles? At the pace we were running now? I didn't know about Henry, but I was pretty sure I'd be experiencing cardiac arrest after four miles.

"Don't be stupid," Henry said easily. "Ten miles is too much this early in the season. No need to risk injuries."

Frank didn't say anything. I looked at him, watched the way his arms and legs pumped like pistons in an engine. He kept his motion tight. Nothing was lost, nothing wasted. Donahue had heard right. Frank was a regular running machine.

"To the lake and back," Henry said finally. "That's ten miles. Is that okay with you?"

I looked at Henry, wondering if maybe he wasn't getting enough oxygen to his brain.

"Don't matter to me," said Frank.

We wheeled down Academy Avenue and turned right on Main Street. We were in the old, tree-lined part of town now. In the thin light of late February most of the houses looked shadowy and tired. I guess they'd seen too much winter—just like me.

"This road will take us to the viaduct," Henry said. I could tell he was trying to control the way his voice sounded. He was trying to cover the fact that his breath—like mine—was coming in short spurts. "After we run under the viaduct, it's straight on to the lake."

Frank didn't say a word. He just kept his easy motion flowing like cream out of a china pitcher. We ran to the viaduct. Somebody had spray-painted something across it in big black letters. WHY DOES IT HAVE TO HURT SO BAD?

"Now, that's something I'd really like to know," I said. By now I was getting a sideache roughly the size of the Grand Canyon. The only way I was going to make ten miles today was on top of a stretcher.

"Hey, guys," I said, "I think I may be developing a serious groin injury here. I'm turning back."

"Later, Marcus," grunted Henry.

Frank didn't say good-bye, which came as no big surprise.

When I got back to school, Donahue asked me how things had gone.

"The guy has a chip on his shoulder the size of a very large boulder," I said.

"Hmmm," said Donahue. He pulled two pieces of Juicy Fruit out of his pocket—one for him, one for me.

"But," I told him, putting the gum in my mouth, "he can definitely run. He's Henry all over again."

Donahue looked at me. "Speaking of guys who can run, Jenkins, I've been watching. You're better than you think you are. And you'll be a whole lot better than that once you get over your habit of fading when Yazzie takes the lead."

I was so surprised, I nearly choked on my gum. Henry was the runner in our family. I was just along for the ride.

"I'm being straight with you, Jenkins," said Donahue. "You've got ability." Then he turned and walked away. I watched him go. But his words stayed in my ears. *You're better than you think you are.*

I went to the locker room, showered, changed my clothes. Henry wasn't back yet. I figured there might be just enough time for me to run to the school library, check out a book I needed, then meet Henry back here.

When I got back to the locker room, I saw him standing in front of the mirror. He was naked except for the white towel wrapped around his middle. Water rolled down his thick black hair straight into his eyes. He was looking at his own reflection like he'd never seen it before.

"Henry?"

He turned, and his eyes caught mine.

"So," I said, "did you and Rambo have a nice little run?"

He just laughed. I sat down on a bench while he got dressed.

"You want to hear something kind of funny?" Henry asked.

"Okay."

"Frank's a Hopi."

I waited for the punch line. "So?" I said finally.

"Hopis basically hate Navahos, Marcus. Hopis think they're better than Navahos. They think they're smarter, better looking, you name it. They think Navaho land belongs to them." Henry was pulling a clean gray sweatshirt over his head. "Don't you just love the irony of it, Marcus? The counselors at his old school send Frank over here because they figure the two of us will hit it right off. An Indian is an Indian is an Indian as far as they're concerned. There is no Navaho, no Hopi, no Ute, no Zuni, no Apache. Just brown skin. Just Indians."

"So what did you say to Frank?"

"I told him that he wasn't on the reservation anymore and that the old rules didn't apply."

"What did he say?"

Henry let out a short, bitter laugh. "I doubt he was listening."

"Jerk," I said. "The guy's a complete jerk."

"You got it." Henry pulled the last of his gear out of his locker. "Can you do a favor for me?"

"What?"

"Cover for me at the theater tonight?"

"Tonight? The Bulls are playing on TV."

"It's Celia," said Henry. "She's invited me to her house."

This little piece of information changed things. Considerably. "Okay, pal," I said. "Just this once."

"HEY, SOLDIER BOY!" Fritz croaked at me when I walked into his office to punch in. "Where's your buddy tonight?"

"He's sick. Gingivitis," I told him while slipping on my velveteen jacket. The jacket was getting too small. This sort of thing happens when you grow four inches in a year.

Fritz looked at me through slitty little eyes. He grunted and handed me a paper from a pile sitting on his desk.

I looked at it. It was a vocabulary list with multiple choice definitions after each word.

"What's this, Fritz?" I asked.

"Hey! That's Mr. Minster to you," scowled Fritz. "Anyway, this word list is from the *Reader's Digest.* They have one of these word deals every month. 'It Pays to Enrich Your Word Power.' I thought it would be a good idea if we all studied these and then passed them off to each other."

"You're giving us homework now?"

Fritz scowled some more.

"Right," I said. "I'll take one for Henry too."

Henry. Who was supposed to pick me up at eleven P.M. but didn't. It was too cold to wait out front, so I had to keep going inside, where I had to listen to Fritz tell me that the Communists were planning to poison the free world's supply of navel oranges.

At one point he started repeating my name to himself out loud. "Marcus Marcus Marcus," he said. "That's a gladiator name, isn't it?"

I just stared at Fritz and I started making a list in my head.

Where They Got Fritz From
1. Out of a cereal box—

Henry showed up just before midnight.

"Hey, pencilneck!" grunted Fritz when he saw the hearse. "I thought you said your buddy was sick."

"Thanks a lot, pal," I said as I crawled into the hearse and slammed the door so I couldn't hear Fritz screaming after us.

"I'm sorry," said Henry.

"Spending an evening with Fritz is like taking a field trip to the Twilight Zone." I was pretty steamed. "By the way, Mom kept calling. I kept telling her we'd be home any minute. You know how crazy she can get."

"I screwed up," said Henry. "I'm sorry."

He really was.

"Forget it," I said. "So tell me about your evening with Celia."

"Well"—he paused—"she *did* invite me up to her bedroom to show me her drawings."

"Oh, right."

Henry was grinning. "I'm serious. Pen and ink, watercolor, oil—Celia does all three. She's really talented."

This was not the kind of information I was interested in. "She does people mostly," he was saying. "Her walls are covered with figure drawings."

"Do they have any clothes on?"

Henry started to laugh. "Shut up."

"Come on," I begged. "Tell me something good."

So he told me how Celia's parents were gone and how they took her Dad's Porsche out for a test drive and how they got followed by a cop but didn't get pulled over and how they laughed about it over pizza later.

"Celia said if life really were like a Sunday School lesson, then we would have gotten pulled over," Henry told me. "Or we would have hit a kid or an old lady in a crosswalk or something like that. We would have been caught and handcuffed and sent to jail. Our lives would have been ruined, just because we took the Porsche without asking first. She said her dad talks like that all the time—if you smoke you'll get lung cancer, if you do drugs you'll OD, if you have sex you'll get AIDS."

He paused. "Then she said, 'I guess he doesn't realize that if you're smart enough you don't have to get caught.'"

"Wow," I said. Just hearing about Henry's evening was enough to drive a person to heavy breathing.

He laughed again and eased back against his seat. "I'm in way over my head, Marcus. Way over."

"Worse things could happen to a guy."

The cold night air whistled through my window. The window crank was missing, so I couldn't do anything about it. I pulled my velveteen jacket tighter around me. I realized I'd left my civilian clothes (as Fritz likes to call them) back at the theater.

So I sat there freezing and thinking about how good things just naturally seemed to happen to Henry. What would it feel like to have a few of them come my way too?

7

TWO WEEKS and Lazarus the cat was already a member of the family. I didn't know how Mom and Dad would react to a cat at first. We had pets once. Julia had two gerbils she kept breeding for science fair projects on Mendel's laws. Actually, Julia didn't have to breed them. They pretty well took care of that for themselves. Those two gerbils kept so busy breeding that there were new gerbils in the cage every time you turned around. We gave the babies (or "gerblettes," as I liked to call them) to Julia's friends, to pet stores, to Diana, to Diana's friends. One day Dad even took some to work with him to see if he could give them away there. When he came home that day he said enough was enough. He made Julia give the gerbils to her teacher for classroom pets. But Mom and Dad liked Lazarus. They're suckers for hard-luck stories.

I woke up late one Saturday morning about two weeks after we found the cat. When I went downstairs (still wearing my boxers and a T-shirt), I found Julia, Mom, and Henry in the kitchen. Mom and Henry were sitting on snack-bar stools. Henry was drinking a glass of orange juice. Mom, as usual, was starting the day off with a can of Coke. Both of them were staring out the kitchen window. Lazarus was curled up like colored yarn in Henry's lap. Julia had the kitchen table covered with colored paper and cardboard, glue and crayons.

"Hi, Sleepyhead!" said Mom.

"Hi, Marcus," Julia said. "Your hair sure looks stupid this morning."

"Oh, thank you very much, Legs. What are you doing there?"

"I'm inventing something wonderful. Our school is having an invention convention."

"What are you inventing?"

She shrugged. "I don't know yet." That's Julia for you. Even when she doesn't know what she's doing, she still knows she's doing it right.

"Come join us," Mom said. "Henry and I were just sitting here watching Diana trying to take poor old Boston on a walk."

I walked over to the window. Diana was walking up the sidewalk very slowly with Boston hobbling alongside. His hind legs were so stiff with arthritis that he could barely move them.

"I wonder how old Boston is," Henry said.

"Oh," Mom said, "he must be thirteen or fourteen years old now. Diana's had him since she was a toddler."

"That dog is in a lot of pain," Henry said, stroking Lazarus behind the ears. "Diana ought to have him put to sleep—it would be kinder than letting him go on like he is right now. Diana should know that better than anybody else."

"True," Mom agreed. "Sometimes it's just hard to let go. Even when you know you should."

"Diana's mom is getting married again this summer," Julia announced out of nowhere. She looked very pleased with herself for telling us all the news. "His name is Tom, only he spells it T-h-o-m."

Henry looked at me and rolled his eyes.

Mom grunted like she'd just been sacked by a couple of linemen. "DeeDee is getting married *again*?" Mom and DeeDee have known each other for a long time. They don't have a whole lot in common, but they like to stand out front with their arms folded and talk about stuff going on in the neighborhood.

"Yup," said Julia.

"How do *you* know, Legs?" I asked her.

"Diana told me a few days ago." Julia loves Diana mainly because Diana talks to her like she's a real human being instead of the squirrely little kid she is.

"I can't believe it." Mom groaned.

I looked out the window again at Diana. The wind was whipping her long red hair across her face. How long would this marriage last? How would Diana's new dad treat her? No doubt he was taking her out to dinner and bringing her presents and asking her about school. But as soon as he and DeeDee got married, he'd probably forget Diana even existed. Her own father isn't much better. He lives overseas and hardly ever sees her.

She stopped and waited for Boston, who was barely moving. She looked like a mom waiting for her little kid. Only, she wasn't one of those grumpy mothers you see downtown who are always screaming at their kids to please hurry up. When Boston finally reached her, Diana bent over and hugged him around the neck, and I knew the look in her eyes said she would take care of him no matter what.

It occurred to me that I'd never seen that look on DeeDee's face.

"Poor Boston," Mom said in a low soft voice. "Poor Diana."

Nobody said anything for a long time. Not even Julia.

After a while Henry started talking to Mom, and I remembered the two tickets to a Utah Jazz basketball game I'd won in a drawing held by a running-shoe store in the mall. It was practically the first time in my life I'd ever won anything.

"Hey, Henry. Wanna go to a Jazz game tonight?" I asked. "They're playing the Lakers."

Henry smiled. "Sounds great, but I'm going out with Celia tonight."

Again.

"Oh," I said. I was surprised by how disappointed I felt. Here I had these two really great tickets nowhere *near* the rafters and Henry couldn't go with me. I felt like a little kid who didn't quite get what he wanted on Christmas morning.

He was looking at me. "Hey, I'm sorry."

I managed to smile. "Forget it. I'd rather be with Celia Cunningham than with me too," I joked.

I could feel Mom turn into her student-social-worker self. She was looking very hard at me and Henry. Any minute now she was going to start asking us leading questions so that we could all open up and share our feelings.

"Have a great time tonight," I said in a hurry. "I'll ask somebody else."

"You could take me, Marcus," Julia suggested.

"You? Ha! I'd rather take Dracula's girlfriend."

"Mo-ther," Julia whined.

"Marcus," Mom warned. But I could tell her heart wasn't in it. My parents think Julia can be a real pain in the rear even though she's flesh of their flesh.

I went upstairs to our room to put on my clothes. Who could I ask to go to the game with me? Diana would say yes in a minute if I had a couple of tickets to watch the Cubs play at Wrigley Field. Unfortunately, she hates basketball.

I thought of Crazy Smitty, who works at the theater. He's a nice enough guy in his own weird way. He's always helping me jump-start the hearse, for example. But sometimes you get the feeling that Crazy Smitty got stuck a couple of rungs behind the rest of us on the way up the old evolutionary ladder. He catches flies and swallows them whole, and once he even put lighter fluid in his belly button, then lit a match just to see what would happen. It's that kind of stuff that makes you worry that it might not be safe to let him loose in a public place without inoculating him for rabies first. Inviting Crazy Smitty was out.

Which left—exactly nobody.

I sat on the edge of my bed and started to pull on a long white sock. To tell you the truth, it was pretty depressing to realize that there wasn't anybody I wanted to invite.

The problem was that I was used to doing everything with Henry—goofing around, going to the mall, watching movies, playing video games, whatever. Now that he was spending most of his spare time with Celia, I was left hanging around alone a lot.

There was probably a really simple trick to hanging out alone. I just hadn't figured out what it was yet. As soon as Celia showed up at our locker every morning, I headed for the magazine rack in the library so I could catch up on back issues of *Mad* magazine.

I looked around for my other sock—under my pillow, under my bed—but I couldn't find it. Have you ever noticed how socks are always getting lost? To me this is one of the life's larger mysteries—right up there with the disappearance of the dinosaurs and the creation of the universe. I started making a list in my head. *What Happens to Socks.*

1. The washing machine eats them.

2. The house eats them.

3. Julia eats them—

The longer I looked for that sock, the worse I felt. I was realizing something that made me feel even stupider than usual. I was realizing that Henry was the one with all the ideas about what we should do and where we should go. He isn't flashy or loud about it. Henry just knows what he likes to do. Me, I don't always care a lot. It's just always been easier to let Henry make the decision, since I pretty much like the things that he likes.

I'm even on the track team because of Henry. Basketball is my favorite sport, but it never occurred to me to try out for the school team. I'd probably get cut the first time around, and I didn't want to see a list on the gym door without my name on it. The only reason I went out for track was because Henry did. Henry told me he was going to try out and said why didn't I? We worked out for a couple of months before, and then we tried out together during the spring of our freshman year. I was amazed when I made it. Sometimes when I'm lying in bed at night I still think about how good it felt when I found out.

Now I remembered what Coach Donahue said to me at practice a couple of weeks ago. I had the words memorized, backward and frontward. *"You're better than you think you are. And you could be a whole lot better than that."* Did he really mean it? But then, I had to admit that Donahue never says anything he doesn't mean. I hadn't told Henry or my parents what he had said. I treated his words like some big secret. The words were for me. They were mine.

I lay on my bed with one sock on and one sock off and thought while I stared at the ceiling. How did I feel?

Lonely, I guess. Mostly lonely.

When I got up, I decided to ask the original Utah

Jazz fan—my dad—if he wanted to go to the game with me. By the end of the evening I'd made up another list called *Ten Good Reasons Why You Should Never Take Your Father on a Date.*

For one thing, he wore his cowboy boots. The guy puts those things on and he thinks he's stinking Louis L'Amour. We also took *his* car to Salt Lake, which meant we had to listen to country-western music all the way up. Then at the game he screamed and shouted at the refs all night long. It's one thing to sit there with a bunch of friends and hammer the refs, but it's another to sit there and listen to your dad do it.

"Did you go to referee school?" I asked him, sounding more annoyed than I wanted to. "Is that why you always know so much more than they do?"

And then I think it's pretty embarrassing the way he sits there and carries on a nonstop conversation with all the people around us like they're long-lost cousins. By the end of the game I was in a really lousy mood.

When we got to the car, Dad flipped on the radio.

"Why oh why," a voice wailed, "did you have to lie? / Did you really wanna make me cry / When all I ever tried to do—"

I reached over and flipped the radio to a rock station, then turned up the volume.

Dad looked at me, then flipped the radio back.

"—was spend my whole life lovin' you?"

"Do we have to listen to this?" I said.

"What's wrong with this?" he asked. "I'd really like to know. You and Henry—you're always on my case."

"Nothing's wrong with it," I said, and then I mumbled under my breath, "if you happen to be a musical moron."

"What was that?" Dad said. "What did you say?"

"Nothing," I practically shouted. Then I folded my arms across my chest and stared out the window. The lights of Salt Lake City streamed past.

"Seriously. I'd like to know why you object to my music."

"Okay, then," I said. "I hate this kind of music because these people are always singing about trains and prison and finding out that your girlfriend is actually sleeping with your brother. These songs are so *depressing.*"

Dad turned off the radio and we drove in silence.

"Well, thanks anyway for the ticket," he said finally.

Suddenly I felt like a real jerk. I'd been acting mad at Dad all night long when it was really myself I was mad at. I was mad at myself because I was the kind of guy who couldn't think of anybody to invite to a stupid basketball game.

"Are you okay?" Dad asked.

"I'm great."

Dad cleared his throat, which is a sign that he wants to have A Talk. "This new girlfriend of Henry's —what's her name again?"

"Celia Cunningham."

"Right. Stan Cunningham's daughter. I've golfed with him. What's she like?"

"She's very good looking."

"Well, I can't say I like her old man much. He's one of these self-made guys who thinks they know everything."

This made me smile. "Not like you—who really do know everything."

"Right, wise guy." Dad smiled too.

We drove for a while longer.

"You and Henry used to do pretty much everything together, but now he's gone a lot. Have any feelings about that?"

"I haven't thought about it."

"Well, maybe it's a good thing that you and Henry are pursuing your own interests more"—I loved it. Calling Celia an interest as though she were a hobby like croquet or stamp-collecting—"because it gives you both a chance to develop and grow. You've been pretty dependent on each other. Especially you, Marcus. Sometimes you hang back."

Obviously, he and Mom had been comparing case notes just like they were Mr. and Mrs. Sigmund Q. Freud.

"Well, excuse me for not inheriting all of your terrific extrovert genes," I said. He was starting to get on my nerves all over again.

"Am I getting on your nerves again?" he asked. Sometimes I think it would be really great to have a father whose vocabulary is limited to grunts and short requests for beer. Sometimes I hate the way Dad can almost read my mind when he wants to. Being a shrink's kid can really stink.

"You're not talking," Dad said.

"Are you going to bill me for this?"

THAT NIGHT after I was already in bed, Henry slipped in late. A hint of perfume tickled my nose.

I rolled over and propped my head up on my hand. "Since when did you start wearing that lovely fragrance?"

He laughed, then lifted his arm and smelled his own skin. I wondered why girls chose one kind of perfume instead of another. Celia's smelled like something blooming on a warm summer night.

"How was the game?" Henry stood by the window and peeled off his clothes in a flood of pale moonlight.

"The Jazz won. Stockton was great. The Mailman delivered. But I'd rather talk about *your* night."

Henry didn't say anything. I watched him fold his clothes like always and put them in his drawers. Naturally, my clothes were lying in a heap at the foot of my bed, and Lazarus was sleeping on top of them.

"Celia's doing a portrait of me," he said slowly.

I tried to imagine Henry sitting motionless, practically holding his breath for Celia while she painted his picture.

"Does it look like you?"

"I don't know," he answered, frowning a little in the half-light. "Maybe it's too early to tell."

I rolled back on my pillow, sliding my hands beneath my head and lacing my fingers together. Was there a girl somewhere who would paint my picture someday? I could still smell Celia's perfume, lingering in our room. I turned over, burying my face in the pillow.

"I still haven't met Celia's parents," said Henry. "Right now they're in Palm Springs because Mr. Cunningham likes to golf. Celia stays by herself when they go out of town."

"Some people have all the luck," I mumbled into my pillow.

Henry crawled into his bed. "She talks about her dad a lot. How strict he is. How he'd kill her if he knew she drives the Porsche when he's gone."

"Sounds like a really great guy."

"Yeah. I can hardly wait to meet him." Sarcasm laced Henry's voice.

"Good night." I rolled back over to get some sleep. But the smell of Celia's perfume kept me awake.

8

THE FIRST DUAL SCHOOL MEET was coming up on Saturday.

I was actually working out pretty hard at practice —doing things the way I was supposed to do them instead of cutting a lot of corners. I kept looking out of the corner of my eye to see if maybe Donahue was watching. Sometimes he was. Which made me work even harder.

Sometimes Frank made it to practice. Sometimes he didn't. Even when he came, I hardly ever saw him. When it came to vanishing into thin air, Frank was a genius. I wondered a lot, though, how he'd actually do in a race. He looked great in practice, but it's a funny thing. Sometimes people who really burn up the track in practice don't do as well in a race. The pressure gets to them. On the other hand, pressure sets some people on fire and they start clocking times you'd never think they were capable of getting. As for Henry—well, Henry looked great all the time.

I was a little worried about him, though. Henry had started running again late at night.

The Shadow Brothers

Henry loves to run at night during the summer. I don't mean dusk or twilight or early evening, but when it's pitch black outside. He wrote a poem about it once called "Star Runner," which is the poem Miss Brett sent to the folks back in New York. I only remember the last two lines:

I weave through the night, run patterns in air
With the moon in my eyes and the stars in my
hair.

But now he was running at night even though it was cold and very black outside. And he was running so hard that you'd almost think he had a ghost at his heels. I couldn't figure it. Why was Henry driving himself so hard? It might have something to do with Frank. He didn't talk about it, but there was definitely something bad brewing between those two. You could feel it whenever they were anywhere near each other.

Meanwhile Henry was working out too hard and too much.

He didn't come home on Thursday night. He had his sweats with him when Diana and I dropped him off at work on our way to the library to do our history class projects. He told us not to worry about picking him up after work because he was planning to change his clothes and run home from the theater.

I expected him home by midnight, but by one A.M. he still hadn't shown up.

I couldn't sleep, so I got out of bed and went downstairs to the kitchen to peel an orange. Maybe Fritz made him stay late, I told myself as I tried to pull the orange apart without maiming it. But then, why hadn't he called to let us know? Maybe he'd gone to Celia's house. At midnight? Don't be completely stupid.

Lazarus walked into the room and started threading himself in and out of my legs. My stomach felt sick and heavy.

"Hey, cat," I said reaching down to scratch him beneath his chin, "I'm real worried."

Lazarus meowed.

I didn't know what to do. I didn't want to wake up my parents, because this is exactly the sort of thing that makes my mother start calling every emergency room in our particular time zone. I had another idea— I could take the hearse and go look for Henry myself.

I looked out the side window and saw Diana's house. Her bedroom light was on, which meant she was probably still finding out more things about the Marshall Plan than anyone needs to know. I decided to call her.

Diana answered the phone.

"It's me, Diana."

"Marcus"—big pause while she checked the digital clock by her bed—"it's one in the morning!"

I loved it. Diana calls whenever she needs me to help her run a rescue—any time, any day, no problem. But the minute I return the favor, she starts acting like I'm a maniac.

"It's Henry," I told her. "He hasn't come home yet."

"Oh, no! Give me a few minutes to get dressed. I'll be right over and then we'll go find him."

I was still looking for the keys when Diana showed up wearing baggy green pants and a huge black sweatshirt.

"I can't find my keys," I said.

"Why don't you ever put them in the same place twice?"

"I don't need you to organize my life for me," I told her. "I already have Julia for that."

Diana started looking, too, swearing under her breath as she rifled through the drawer under the telephone. It was mostly full of old Popsicle sticks and pens that didn't work.

"Henry could be hurt. He could be lying somewhere out there in the middle of the road and we're stuck here looking for your damn keys!" Any minute now Diana was going to lower her head and paw the ground. I was beginning to wonder why I'd even called her in the first place.

Just then Henry shoved open the kitchen door and limped inside, his face twisted in pain.

Diana raced to him, lifted his arm over her shoulders, and helped him to a chair.

"I slipped on some ice," Henry said in a tight voice. "I think I sprained my ankle."

"I'll get Dad," I said.

I woke my parents up and they followed me down the stairs without even bothering to throw robes on first. I noticed for the millionth time how funny they both look when they first get out of bed. Sometimes I think it's pretty amazing that a lot of married people still love each other even though they have to look at each other first thing in the morning.

Dad started packing Henry's ankle with ice right away.

"I want you to look at Henry," Mom said to Dad. "Observe how calm he is in spite of the pain. Unlike you, Carl, he isn't a boob when he's hurt."

"I am not a boob," said Dad as he felt Henry's ankle for swelling. "I just didn't particularly appreciate it that time you backed over my foot."

Mom drove over Dad's foot while they were on their honeymoon and they never let each other forget it.

"Are you okay, Henry?" Dad asked.

"Yeah," he said.

Mom and Dad exchanged a look. Something told me they were worried about Henry and that they had been worried about him before tonight. Just like me. Realizing this made me feel even worse. It was like being a little kid and telling your mom you're afraid to go to sleep because there's a vampire in the closet and having her say "You're right. There really *is* a vampire in your closet."

"I can't believe you got yourself home on that thing," said Mom, putting an arm around Henry's shoulder and touching his hair with her free hand.

I tried to crack a little joke, which is what I always do whenever I'm nervous or uncomfortable. Or scared. "He's got bionic ankles," I said. Nobody laughed.

"Will I be able to run in Saturday's meet?" Henry asked.

There was a little silence and then everyone— Mom, Dad, Diana—started talking at the same time.

"Don't be stupid—" said Diana.

"Absolutely not—" said Mom.

"I think you'd better hold off—" said Dad.

Henry looked at me. You know how it is when you know someone so well you can practically think their thoughts for them? I could *feel* his complete and total frustration. He'd have to wait.

He'd have to wait before he could go head-to-head with Frank.

We showed up early at the meet on Saturday morning. Henry was decked out in bandage and crutches. I had on my track suit and warm-ups.

"Well, what do you know," Henry said. I followed his eyes. Frank was stretching out on the far side of the field.

"He decided to show," I said. "Very big of him."

Henry walked across the field.

"Let it alone, Henry."

But he ignored me, so I followed him.

Henry just stood there, casting a long shadow over Frank, who looked up and grunted.

"Nervous?" asked Henry.

Frank laughed. "Nervous? About running against guys like him?" He nodded in my direction.

"Thanks," I said.

Henry narrowed his eyes and spoke in a low angry voice that was almost a growl.

"Listen, pal," he said, "I'm going to tell you something I should have told you a long time ago. You've got a real attitude problem, know that? There've been plenty of people here who've bent over backward to help you when you didn't much deserve it."

"Anglos," Frank snorted.

"Right. Anglos," Henry said. "Anglos who've tried their best to help you fit in here."

Frank stood up so that his face wasn't much more than six inches away from Henry's face. "Maybe I don't want to fit in."

Frank certainly had a gift for stating the obvious. Henry and Frank glared at each other.

"We got a *name* for boys like you where I come from," said Frank. His voice was real soft. "We call boys like you apples."

Henry looked as surprised as I felt. He had no idea what Frank was talking about.

"Wow," said Henry. "I'm wounded, Chief. Seriously."

"Red on the outside. White on the inside. Apple."

Henry looked at Frank. Then he did exactly the right thing. He laughed right in Frank's sneering face.

Frank turned and trotted off.

"See you later, Apple," Frank called over his shoulder.

"Maybe we should go rearrange his face," I said.

"The guy isn't worth the trouble," said Henry. And he laughed again, but he didn't take his eyes off Frank for a second.

By the time the call came for the mile, I was pretty

nervous. Usually I figure if I don't finish last then I'm doing okay, but today I wanted to do better. I felt like Donahue was watching me with those gray eyes of his. I felt like he was counting on me.

The milers stood together in a pack. There was some last-minute jostling and bumping. I felt an elbow in my ribs. When I turned, I saw Frank by my side. He wasn't looking at me, but I was pretty sure he'd thrown the elbow at me on purpose. *Forget it,* I told myself. I swallowed and my throat felt thick and dry.

The second call came. Everyone got ready.

The gun went off.

No kidding. I shot off like I was on fire. For the first two laps it was just me and Frank together at the front of the pack. But then I started to fade. I didn't have the base to carry off my quick start. Not yet.

Frank pulled away easily. Then another runner passed me. I had no kick whatsoever on the backstretch. I hung on but my legs burned and my lungs felt like they would explode. At the very last second a third runner stepped over the finish line before I did.

Fourth place.

I swore under my breath and closed my eyes so tight that my eyelids quivered. Everything hurt—my throat, my chest, my thighs. When I coughed, I thought I tasted blood.

Fourth stinking place.

I took a cool-down lap and then stepped onto the grass, where I bent over and caught my breath. I went to check my time.

My time, at least, was a whole lot better than my place.

"It was a pretty fast heat," said Donahue, coming up behind me. "That happens sometimes when you throw a kid like Frank in there."

I turned around and looked at him.

"We'll work on that start of yours," Donahue said. Then he popped a stick of gum in his mouth and smiled at me a little—Donahue doesn't believe in big grins—and he walked away.

I didn't win. I didn't even place. But I didn't show Donahue he'd been wrong about me, either, and that was saying something. Maybe there was hope for me yet.

Henry hobbled up to me as I was pulling on my warm-up suit. I waited for him to congratulate me on my race.

"Frank can run," he said. He folded his arms and stared at Frank, who was standing by himself on the other side of the field.

"Yeah," I said. "He can."

Neither of us said anything for a minute. I listened to the wind whip the flag around the flagpole.

"I should have been out there, Marcus," Henry said. "That should have been *my* race."

I'd been hoping that it would have been my race, but I didn't say anything.

"I'm going to beat him, Marcus," Henry said very quietly. "I'm going to make him sorry he ever came here."

Henry moved away from me then, thinking his own thoughts.

I watched Henry limp away and I tried to understand for the millionth time why he seemed to hate Frank as much as he did. True, Frank wasn't the most lovable human being in the world, but it was very strange that he had managed to get under Henry's skin in such a big way.

I doubted that Henry hated Frank because he was Hopi and Henry was Navaho. That was Frank's fight, not Henry's. And I didn't think Henry hated Frank because he was afraid Frank could run faster—Henry certainly had more class than that. So what was the problem? Why couldn't Henry just dismiss Frank as the big nothing he obviously was?

A gust of wind nearly blew right through me, making the bones in my face ache. There was something else I didn't get either. Henry was disappointed about the way things had turned out today. Okay. I understood that. But you think he could have at least congratulated *me* on *my* race.

I pulled up the hood of my sweatshirt and followed Henry across the field. Sometimes it seemed like I was *always* following Henry somewhere. A crumpled paper cup skipped toward me across the grass. I tried to kick it out of my way but missed it completely.

9

I HAVE THIS THEORY.

I think you can tell a lot about someone's personality just by looking at the inside of their school locker. Henry's side of our locker is clean and well organized. There are no stray papers or gym shoes, no candy wrappers or old school newspapers, no stale doughnuts or overdue library books. Just his letterman's jacket and his backpack. Also, the books on Henry's shelf are stacked very neatly—big books on the bottom of the pile, little books on top. My side of the locker, on the other hand, looks a little like my side of our room at home. Lived in.

I bent down to hunt for my math assignment.

"Hi, Marcus," Henry said.

I stood up quickly and bumped my head on the lower shelf for the thousandth time this year.

"Ouch!" someone said for me, then laughed. I turned around and saw Celia looking mighty fine in a white sweater and a white pair of pants.

"Hi, Marcus," she said.

I smiled at her, then looked at Henry. "Have you seen my math assignment?

"The one due today?"

I nodded.

Henry smiled a little. "I don't think you got around to doing it."

I let out a big fake sigh. "I was afraid of that."

"I hate math," said Celia.

"Listen to *her*." Henry was really grinning now. "She only got an A in algebra last semester."

Celia shrugged away Henry's comment. "It wasn't hard, just pointless. I'll never use it in real life."

"That's very true," I said. "The only math anybody uses in real life is story problems."

Normally I don't say much around girls I don't know, but since Celia and I were actually saying hello to each other in the halls these days, I thought I'd try joking around with her.

"Story problems?" she repeated. Henry was looking at me in surprise. He knows how shy I am around girls except for Diana.

"Let me give you an example of a two-part story problem that you can use in real life, Celia," I said, warming up to the subject. "Say you have forty-seven pairs of shoes. Your best friend has fifty pairs of shoes. The first question is, who has more pairs of shoes—you or your friend—and the second question is, should you hate her for it." I started to break up until I saw Celia's face.

She wasn't even smiling. Instead she looked like she felt a little sorry for me.

"I was just kidding." My face turned red. "I really don't know how many pairs of shoes you have."

That's not what I'd meant to say but the damage was done. Henry was looking at me over Celia's shoulder like I was crazy. I wanted to crawl into my locker and slam the door permanently behind me. I thought of a title for another soon-to-be-completed list: *How to Feel like an Idiot Without Really Trying*.

Just then somebody bumped Henry from behind.

I don't think Frank did it on purpose. At first he had a real surprised look on his face. But when he saw Henry, his expression turned nasty.

I watched them square off. They both had good-looking, strong-featured faces and the exact same runner's build—medium height, long legs, lean arms and chest. But Henry was wearing a long-sleeved white cotton T-shirt and a pair of faded but very clean Levi's, both of which he had ironed the night before. Frank was wearing a cheap pair of jeans—a brand that no one around here wears—and an old denim jacket. He also had on a pair of cowboy boots. Frank needed a haircut. Bad.

Celia started inching closer to Henry.

"This your girlfriend?" Frank slowly looked Celia up and down.

"Get out of here," Henry said.

Frank held up his hands. "Hey," he said with an ugly smile, "I don't want no trouble."

Frank took one last look at Celia. "See you later, Apple," he said. Then he walked away.

"What does he mean by that?" Celia wanted to know.

"Nothing," said Henry.

Frank strutted down the hall.

"That guy has got one cocky walk," I said.

"Are they *all* like that where he comes from?" asked Celia.

I looked at her in surprise. Couldn't she hear how stupid her question sounded?

Henry stared at her, too, and for just a second he looked like he didn't even like her very much. "No, Celia. Not everyone who lives on a reservation is like that. Frank is just one person."

Henry's voice was pure ice, but I don't think she even noticed.

"I guess we'd better go," she said.

"See you guys later," I said.

Henry placed his hand in the small of Celia's back and guided her down the hall. I watched them until they turned the corner.

Maybe it was because she hadn't laughed at my joke about the shoes or maybe it was because I hated getting left out all the time now. But the truth was I didn't know what I thought about Celia.

I just didn't know.

IT WAS MAYBE NINE P.M. OR SO. Henry was out and I was stretched on my bed reading *Tarzan and the Ant Men*. I was also wishing that Miss Brett would let us do a paper on a book of our choice instead of *Moby*

Dick. That way at least I wouldn't have to check out the video.

The phone rang.

"Marcus," Mom called, "it's for you."

I picked up the phone in our room.

It was Diana. "I just got another crisis call. Can you help me out again? Please?"

"Well," I said, "since you said please this time—"

There was sharp click, then a buzz in my ear. One thing about Diana—she sure doesn't fool around with small talk.

"Mom," I yelled, "Diana needs me to help her. Okay with you?"

"Okay with me!" Her voice drifted back up to me.

I pulled on my jacket and ran outside. Diana was striding the distance between her house and mine. She was wearing the green wool cape she'd received for Christmas.

"Somebody called and said they saw a dog hit in front of the high school. The car drove off."

"Swell," I said. "A dog homicide."

Diana and I got in the hearse and I drove as fast as I dared to the school. A thick fog was hanging over the valley and it was practically impossible to see.

"North end," Diana said, nervously scanning the road ahead. "There! I see the dog up there."

The headlights picked up a medium-sized black dog lying on the side of the road. It was still.

Diana flew out of the hearse as soon as we came to a stop. She dropped by the side of the dog and ran her hand across its muzzle. I got out and leaned down beside her.

The dog lay half on the sidewalk, half on the gutter. It looked like it had been thrown. The eyes were wide open and shone in the headlights like bits of brown glass. Nothing was crushed or cut, but dark gooey blood oozed from the side of its open mouth.

Slowly Diana stood up. "He's dead." Her voice was trembling.

I felt like a complete jerk for my remarks about a dog homicide. "It probably didn't feel a thing."

Her eyes found mine. "But what if he did?"

Diana looked down at the dog, then straight ahead. Would she cry?

No. She became very businesslike. "Well, we can't leave him here."

For one really grim second I thought she was going to ask if we could take the dog with us. I finally worked up the nerve and asked, "What do you want to do with it?"

Diana looked around, then pointed to an empty field down the street. "There. I'll take him there for tonight. Then I'll call Animal Control first thing in the morning. They'll send someone out to pick him up."

I looked at the dog and felt my stomach shift. An hour ago it had been alive—chasing cats, going through garbage cans, sniffing bushes, doing dog things. Now it was dead, sleek and black and still as coal. I didn't think I could touch it without throwing up.

But she didn't ask for my help.

Instead she crouched down and scooped the dog into her arms. Slowly she stood up. Then she started moving down the street toward the open field, the mist chasing her heels. She began to sing.

"Amazing Grace / how sweet the sound / that saved a wretch like me. . . ."

A funny thing happened to me the minute she started to sing. I stopped breathing.

"I once was lost but now I'm found. . . ."

I had known Diana for years. Next to Henry, she was my oldest friend. You'd think that would mean I'd know everything about her, right? You'd think there wouldn't be any mysteries left. But I'd never known she could sing.

"I was blind, but now I see. . . ."

Her voice was nothing like you'd expect either. Looking at her, you'd figure she'd have a real deep, throaty sort of voice. But her voice is strong, and it's high. It's pure. It haunts you after the song is over.

I just stood there in the middle of the road like an idiot watching her, listening to her sing. With all that wild red hair and that green cape she looked like something out of a myth—a witch, a Valkyrie, a mermaid.

The fog swallowed her and left only her song behind.

"O Lord, I was blind but now I see. . . ."

I was shivering like crazy. And it wasn't just from the cold.

When Diana returned, she had stopped singing.

We got into the hearse together. I started the engine and turned on the heat full blast.

"I didn't know you could sing," I said, my voice sounding very strange.

She shrugged. "Everybody sings."

"Not like that, they don't," I muttered. Then I flipped on the radio and turned it way up loud. I didn't trust myself to talk.

I kept looking at her sideways so she wouldn't know. What else didn't I know about her? Was it possible that you could live so close to a person and not know things—big things—about them?

"Mind if we drive around for a while?" My voice still had a faraway sound.

She looked surprised, then said, "Okay. Mom won't notice if I'm gone tonight." Which meant that DeeDee was drinking again.

We drove slowly through the streets of Lake View —past houses whose lights burned a hazy yellow, past gas stations and 7-Elevens, past Pioneer Park in the old part of town, past the theater where Fritz was probably busy running off copies of "It Pays to Enrich Your Word Power." No doubt it was just the fog, but the town where I'd lived all my life looked suddenly different to me.

I turned the radio off. "I have a confession to make. I've always thought you were a little crazy when it comes to animals."

"You and Henry both. Only, you don't think I'm a little crazy. You think I'm completely nuts. I've seen the way you two exchange looks."

She was right. What could I say? Henry and I thought she hadn't noticed just because she'd been too polite to say anything about it.

"It's just that I feel *so* strongly about things," Diana was saying. "It's true that things die. Plants, animals, people—they all die. And sometimes you think, what's the point? You think that life really is cheap. But it's not." She looked at me straight, her eyes burning. "It's not! We can save it from being cheap. We *decide* to care and by caring we make life—any life—valuable!"

When Diana gets like this, you usually want to start giving her the time-out signal. But tonight I thought her intensity made her—I don't know—beautiful somehow.

"Well, anyway," I mumbled, "I just wanted you to know that I thought you were really something tonight."

Her eyes widened and then her face relaxed into a soft smile, the first one I'd seen tonight. "That's nice of you to say, Marcus." The air hummed when she said my name.

We drove around for a little more and then I dropped her off in front of her house. I watched her run up the stairs, her hair tumbling around her shoulders. She turned to wave at me before slipping through the front door.

From the way my heart was beating, you'd have thought I'd just run a race.

10

I COULDN'T BELIEVE IT.

I'd heard Diana singing in the fog, and now I saw her with totally different eyes. At school, at home, at work—I couldn't stop thinking about her.

I started noticing all sorts of things about her. Like her eyes, for example. She has big green eyes with little gold flecks in them. I also noticed the way she holds her head to one side when she's listening to you and the way she plays with her hair without even knowing she's doing it. I realized how much I like the way her perfume makes the hearse smell in the mornings. I thought I liked Celia's perfume, but Diana's is actually much nicer.

The truth is I had a hard time breathing when she was around.

Could she tell? Feeling like this about Diana was a pretty high-risk venture: she'd probably slug me if she found out.

A few days after finding the dog in front of the high school, we were eating lunch together in the cafeteria, and I could tell she was in a pretty lousy mood.

"What's the matter with you?" Good sign. My voice sounded reasonably normal.

"It's my mother." She grumbled and let out a big sigh. "You know, I really do try to please her. I get good grades. I don't do drugs. I'm nice to old people. But does that matter? No! What matters is that I don't have a date to the Spring Fling!"

"No date, huh?" I acted very casual.

Diana snorted. "Are you kidding? Guys don't like me, Marcus."

"Oh, I don't think that's true," I said. "I think maybe they're just—you know—terrified of you."

Diana looked at me.

"I mean that as a compliment," I added in a hurry.

She lifted an eyebrow, then sank back against her chair. "Sometimes I think my mother wouldn't care if I were an ax murderer as long as I could be prom queen too."

I didn't say anything, but I had an idea. Only, I didn't know if I actually had the guts to go through with it or not. I wanted to talk to Henry first.

I was still thinking about my idea the next morning in the bathroom when Henry and I were getting ready for school. Henry was brushing his teeth while I was very busy looking in the mirror for signs of facial hair.

"Hey, look there." I pointed at my chin. "What do you think about that?"

Henry squinted. "I think it's lint from your sweatshirt."

"Fritz once told me he was shaving twice a day by the time he was in the fourth grade."

Henry laughed and spit out the last of his toothpaste. "I'm surprised he didn't tell you he was born with a beard."

"Are you taking Celia to the Spring Fling?" I asked.

"Yeah." For a guy who was going to a dance with Celia Cunningham, Henry didn't look too happy.

"What's the matter?"

Henry opened the drawer and pulled out a comb. "I'm finally going to be meeting her parents." He started combing his hair slowly. He acted like he had something on his mind, so I waited for him to talk.

"What are you guys doing in there?" It was Julia outside the door.

"What do you think people usually do in a bathroom?" I yelled at her. Then I dropped my voice to a whisper so Julia wouldn't hear.

"What would you say if I told you I was kind of thinking about asking Diana to the dance?"

Henry practically dropped the comb. *"Diana?"*

"Yeah," I said a little defensively, "Diana. She doesn't have a date and neither do I. I thought I'd do her a favor and get DeeDee off her back because I'm such a nice guy." I shrugged like it was no big deal. "I just wondered what you thought."

Henry was looking at my face closely. "I guess I don't know what to think. Since when have you had a thing for Diana?"

"Hey, I don't have a *thing* for Diana. Maybe I'm

just getting a little sick of hanging around the house while you're out eating hamburgers every night with Princess Celia."

Henry's eyes flashed fire and for a split second I thought he might flatten me.

"Hurry up, you guys!" The sound of Julia's voice broke the tension.

"Get lost, Legs," I screamed at her. Then I turned to Henry. "I'm sorry. That was a very stupid thing for me to say."

"Forget it. It was my fault." He paused. "I guess I'm just thinking that this probably will change things for the three of us—you, me, Diana."

"How?" I demanded.

"It's been the three of us for such a long time. But now maybe three will be a crowd. Maybe I'll feel like a third wheel around you guys."

I couldn't believe my ears. It wasn't as though we were the cozy little trio we used to be. That had changed the moment he and Celia Cunningham locked eyeballs over a can of Diet Pepsi in the school cafeteria.

I picked up my comb and tried to pull a snarl out of my hair. "Ouch!"

Henry looked at me. "I don't know what my problem is today. I'm being a jerk. I think it would great if you asked Diana to the dance."

"Well, thank you very much for your permission, Doctor," I snapped.

I felt the back of my neck start to burn, the way it

always does when I get mad. I was mad at Henry. Mad at myself. Mad at Julia for banging on the bathroom door. Mad at Diana for singing in the fog.

I was mad at the way that everything was changing.

I ASKED DIANA to go to the dance with me when we were eating lunch, although *ask* is probably too strong a word. I mumbled the invitation into my chow mein.

"What?" she said. "I can't hear you."

I spoke louder. "Do you want to go to the Spring Fling with me?"

Her mouth dropped open. Then she glanced around the lunchroom like she was looking for hidden cameras.

"Is this a joke?" she asked. "Is Henry hiding under the table?"

"No," I said, acting pretty offended. "This is not a joke. I want you to go to the dance with me."

"Why?"

Why? Because I want to touch your hair and smell your skin and feel the way you move when we dance. I want to look straight into your eyes—

"Marcus? What's the matter?"

"Nothing. I just—remembered something I need to do one day." I smiled weakly.

Diana studied me and then she sat up straight and threw out her chin. "Okay. I'll go with you."

She sounded just like she was accepting a dare.

∘ ∘ ∘

HENRY AND I MADE PLANS that night at the theater. We were working behind the concession counter where I asked customers if they would like a little synthetic butter with their synthetic popcorn. Henry manned the pickle jar and hot-dog grill while Crazy Smitty sat out front in the ticket booth howling at a full moon.

"We could double," I suggested. It would be nice to have Henry around for moral support.

I threw a piece of popcorn about five feet up in the air and caught it with an open mouth. This is one of Crazy Smitty's tricks, only he barks like a seal and claps his flippers when he catches a piece.

"I guess we could." Henry sounded doubtful.

The tone of his voice annoyed me. "If you don't want to double, just say so."

"I want to double. I *live* to double. Okay?" he snapped.

"Fine," I snapped back.

Henry made himself a plate of nachos and smothered them with diced chilis. Whenever I eat that many chilis I feel like I'm lighting a fire inside my head.

"One day you are going to fry your brains, and then where will you be?" I said, but Henry didn't laugh. "Gee. You're in a terrific mood tonight."

"I've got a lot on my mind." He was frowning.

"So, what do you think—dinner first?"

"Yes. Dinner first is a very good idea."

"How about China Village?" China Village is our

family's favorite restaurant. It looks like a real dive, but the food is great. Dad has this theory about Mexican and Chinese restaurants. The worse a place looks, the better its food tastes.

"China Village? I was thinking of someplace a little fancier, someplace that doesn't have a prominently displayed CASH ONLY sign."

"The Spring Fling isn't the Junior Prom, Henry. I don't see the point in blowing a hundred bucks for dinner. Especially when I don't have a hundred bucks."

I knew Henry didn't have a hundred bucks, either, since he'd started seeing Celia. These days Henry was going through cash fast, mainly because he thinks guys still ought to pay for dates. In some ways, Henry is pretty traditional.

"I just wish there wasn't a stuffed moose head on the wall there," Henry said.

It is true that China Village does have a real moose head on the wall.

"I'll hang my coat over it," I said. "Celia will never know it's there."

"Fine," said Henry. "But let's not take the hearse."

I just stared at him. "Remember what I said when we first saw it? Remember how I said I wanted a Camaro with a T-top so that live girls would go for rides with me? But no. *You* said it had possibility."

"Just this once, Marcus. Let's take the Boss's car."

Henry was getting on my nerves in a major big-time way. The hearse was good enough for me. It was good enough for Diana. It was good enough for Henry. But not for Celia.

I didn't know what was happening to him. The Henry I knew B.C. (Before Celia) didn't worry too much about what other people thought. Now he was standing here wondering if he dared to eat at China Village or take the hearse on a date.

"We'll take Dad's car, Henry. Okay?"

Just then Fritz poked his head out of his office door.

"Hey, pinhead!"

"Yo!" I said.

"Can the sweet nothings. No talking on duty. *Comprendo?*"

For once I was more than pleased to obey one of Fritz's orders.

11

HENRY WAS TOO SICK the next morning to go to school. He lay on his bed with his arm across his face.

"I told you to lay off those chilis last night."

He groaned, then chucked his pillow at me. It clipped the side of my head, making my hair stand straight up like fins. I swore and hurled the pillow back into his face. He laughed, then started to cough so hard that his shoulders shook.

"You sound terrible. Better take care of yourself." Before I left I turned the stereo on for him so he wouldn't have to get out of bed.

"WHERE'S HENRY TODAY?" Miss Brett asked after English class.

"Sick."

She tapped her long glazed fingernails on her desk, looking like she was trying to make up her mind about something.

"I want to talk to you in my office," she finally said.

I was surprised to see that her office was almost as

big a mess as my side of the locker. Who would have figured that Miss Brett and I would have something like that in common? There were piles of books and boxes of files everywhere—in the corners, on the floors, in the chair where I would have sat if there'd been enough room. Instead I just stood in the middle of her office, looking at the posters on her walls. Most of them were travel posters, showing cities from around the world—Paris, London, Florence.

One of the posters was different than the rest. It had words written across it: "If a man does not keep pace with his companions, perhaps it is because he hears a different drummer. Let him step to the music which he hears, however measured or far away."

"Thoreau," said Miss Brett, following my gaze. "It's one of his most famous statements."

"Oh," I said in a flat voice. "How interesting."

Miss Brett looked at me like I'd just crawled out from underneath a rock somewhere. "I wanted to ask you about Henry."

Naturally.

"He's okay, isn't he?"

I nodded.

Miss Brett drew her eyebrows together and bit one of her knuckles. "I'm a little concerned about Henry right now. He's not doing his homework. He hasn't handed in a thing for the last two weeks."

What did she expect me to say? I looked at my watch. I was going to be late for my next class.

"Do you know if he's doing *any* writing at all?"

Since Henry only wrote poems when no one was

around, it was kind of hard to answer her question. But I doubted he was. Between school and work, track and Celia, he didn't have a whole lot of time.

I shrugged.

"I get the feeling that something is bothering Henry right now," Miss Brett said. "I wish I knew what it was." She looked straight at me.

I couldn't believe it. Miss Brett wanted me to discuss Henry with her. What kind of a friend did she think I was?

"Henry's fine," I said, returning her stare. "I gotta go now."

"Just a minute, Marcus. I want to talk to you about your report on *Moby Dick*." She riffled through a stack of papers on the corner of her desk until she found mine. It had a big fat F scrawled across the top.

Miss Brett drilled holes through me with her eyes. "When you say here that Captain Ahab looks just like Gregory Peck, it makes me wonder if you just watched the video instead of reading the book."

But that was a joke, I wanted to tell her. *That's just me, Marcus T. Jenkins, listening to my own drummer. You would have realized that by now if you had ever bothered to learn something about me.*

"You must think I am very stupid indeed," she said, handing me my paper with its lovely F.

But isn't that what you think of me? Don't you think I'm stupid? My face grew hot as I folded the paper and jammed it in my back pocket. *Well, in case you're interested, Miss Brett, I'm bored. Maybe I'm even a little lazy.*

But I'm not stupid.

"You ought to read that saying on your poster again," I said with my heart pounding in my ears. "The one by Thoreau."

I expected her to tell me that I ought to arrange an immediate transfer from her class first thing tomorrow morning.

Instead she turned to look at the words on her wall as I slipped through her office door.

AT FIRST it felt *great* to have said something like that to Miss Brett, but after eating lunch, I started to feel pretty stupid.

Okay. So maybe Miss Brett didn't exactly appreciate me as an individual. But then, I really never did any of the things *she* thought were important either. Like reading *Moby Dick*. Who could blame her if she thought I was a moron?

I took the essay out of my back pocket and looked at it again.

F.

It suddenly occurred to me that getting lousy grades in English was so *unnecessary*. I wadded up my paper and threw it with a perfect arc into a garbage can as I walked through the library door.

The student librarian at the circulation desk gave me a dirty look and I was amazed at how much she looked like a high-school version of Julia.

"If you throw any more garbage in here, I'll have to ask you to leave," she said through tight lips. Just like Julia.

"Right," I said. I went to the magazine rack where I picked up a *Mad* magazine and gave it a little flip in the air—just to bug her. Then I took a seat and started to read. It was an old issue that I'd already read at least twenty times. I could practically say all the jokes in my sleep.

I felt someone take a seat nearby. I looked up.

Frank was sitting across from me, looking at *Sports Illustrated*.

This certainly was my lucky day.

I turned the page of my magazine. Obviously Frank hadn't seen me or he would never have sat down. I waited for him to realize he'd made a mistake, then leave.

"Are you going to practice today?" he asked.

I looked up. Was Frank actually saying something to me? "Yeah. Since I *am* on the track team, I guess I'll show up." I buried my nose in my magazine again.

"That stupid coach, he don't know nothing."

Did he want to start a fight right here in the library?

"I guess that's your opinion," I grunted.

"He don't know half as much as my old coach."

I put my magazine down and looked straight at Frank. "Donahue was All-American. Twice. He ran with Jim Ryun. He nearly qualified for the sixty-eight Olympic team. I'm just telling you all this so you'll know. Okay?"

Frank didn't say anything, so I picked up my magazine again. He leafed through the *Sports Illustrated*, pretending to look at the pictures.

"That lady where I live now, she cooks like shit," he said.

"Yeah?" I didn't know what else to say.

"Every meal we have Jell-O. Jell-O with fruit. Jell-O with carrots. Jell-O with little marshmallows."

I had to smile a little. When my parents were first married, Dad used to tease Mom that Jell-O was the Official Food of the Mormon church because you can always find at least twelve varieties of Jell-O salads at church dinners.

"Does she even make you eat Jell-O for breakfast?" I asked.

Frank surprised me by smiling for just a second. He looked like a completely different person when his teeth showed. That didn't last very long—the smile was replaced by a sneer.

"Your friend don't look so good to me in practice," he said.

I didn't answer. Henry was starting to work out again, but he did look a little weak. I wondered how long it would take him before he got everything back.

"I sprained my ankle once and I ran on it the next day," Frank said.

"I'm really thrilled for you." Why didn't he just go away?

I flipped through my magazine and so did Frank. Anybody seeing us from a distance would have probably thought we were pals. A couple of guys hanging out together in the library during lunch hour.

Frank didn't budge from his seat. "You got a sister?" he asked.

"Unfortunately."

"I got a letter from mine yesterday. She wants me to come home." There was no change in Frank's voice or expression. He just kept thumbing through his magazine. But now I understood why he was sitting here complaining to me about Jell-O salads with marshmallows instead of just going away.

Frank was lonely.

He didn't like me and I didn't like him, but at least I was someone who knew his name. For just a split second I felt sorry for him.

I knew something about lonely myself.

12

IF I EVER HAVE TO WRITE an essay entitled "My Most Uncomfortable Date Ever," the Spring Fling will be my inspiration.

Julia did her usual stupid best to get the night off to a great start. As Henry and I were walking out the front door to pick up Diana and Celia, Julia called down the stairway after us.

"Hey, Marcus! Are you going to kiss Diana tonight?"

"Go drown yourself, Legs."

Julia sighed. "I told Diana not to hold her breath waiting. I told her you never kiss girls for real anyway because you're too shy. You just pretend you're kissing girls upstairs all the time in your bedroom."

For the record, I do not kiss pretend girls in my bedroom.

"That's just swell, Julia. Do you want to know how that makes me sound? Like a pervert. Now Diana thinks she's going out with a pervert." I thought about rearranging Julia's braces.

For some reason Dad, who was sitting on the couch

reading the newspaper, seemed to find all this very funny.

"That's right. Go ahead and laugh," I said.

"Have a good time, you guys," he said while digging into his pocket. He tossed Henry the keys to his Chevy.

"Come on," said Henry, who was smiling too.

Laughing, I said to myself, *the whole world is laughing at you tonight, Marcus T. Jenkins.*

I slammed the front door after us.

"Forget Julia," Henry said.

"Look, I just happen to be a little sensitive about the subject of kissing girls, okay? Unlike you, I don't have a lot of recent experience in that area."

"Maybe you'll get lucky tonight." Henry smiled again.

"Oh, right." I wondered for a minute what Diana would do if I tried to kiss her.

"You get Diana and I'll be warming up the engine."

The short walk over to Diana's house gave me plenty of time to realize that my heart was busy leaping up into my throat. Why was I doing this?

For the first time ever in recorded history I opened Diana's front gate and walked through instead of jumping over it. She came out of the house before I got to the porch.

This is an exact quote of what I said when I saw her.

"Wow."

Diana had on a dress, which was unusual in itself,

but the big news was that she looked great in it. It was green and she wore her hair down so it sort of spilled all over her shoulders. Which were bare.

She looked worried. Maybe because she thought she was going out with a pervert.

"Let's go before my mother invites you inside." She hurried down the stairs, then tripped. I caught her arm so that she didn't fall. "Damn! I hate heels!"

"I think they look nice," I said, noticing how much I liked having her so close to me. "I think *you* look nice."

Diana looked straight up into my eyes.

Henry honked. I let go of her arm and Diana smoothed her dress.

"Let's hurry!" She ran to the car, her red hair flying after her. I ran too. As we were pulling away from the curb, DeeDee came out onto the porch in a bathrobe and started yelling something after us.

For a split second Diana looked out the rear window. Then she turned around and closed her eyes.

What a lousy thing, I thought, *to have your mother drunk.*

Henry turned on the radio. Naturally it was on a country-western station, so he found something better. Before long we were at Celia's house. Every single light was on, which is something that never happens at home.

"Now, *this* would drive Dad crazy," I said. "He thinks leaving a light on after you've left the room is a capital offense. Right, Henry?"

Diana laughed.

"I don't need this from you guys." Henry got out of the car and slammed the door.

"Boy, is he touchy," I said.

Diana's eyes followed Henry up the driveway. "He's nervous because he's meeting Celia's parents for the first time tonight."

That explained why he wanted to take Dad's car instead of the hearse. I was surprised I hadn't figured that out for myself the other night at the theater when Henry was being so weird about everything.

We watched him hike up the front stairs and stand in front of the double doors. Somebody opened one of them, and he walked inside.

"I like your dress," I told Diana.

"Do you?" She sounded pretty miserable. "My mother bought it for me. I'd never buy a dress like this for myself."

I smiled a little. For once in her life Diana probably hadn't known what to wear, so DeeDee got to choose something. No doubt she thought she'd died and gone to heaven.

Diana touched one of her shoulders like she was nervous about it being bare. It's a funny thing. On the one hand Diana has enough confidence to stand up to the toughest teacher in the school and tell him she won't dissect one of his stupid frogs. On the other hand she has a real complex about the way she looks. I wished I could make her see how pretty she really is.

She gave a nervous little laugh. I gave a nervous little laugh back.

It's very strange how you can know somebody forever and talk to them about everything and anything. But the minute you start liking them, you can't think of a thing to say. I stared out the window.

Somebody opened the front door and a man came out. He waved at us, then motioned for us to join him.

"I don't want to go inside." Diana sniffed. But she followed me out of the car.

"Hello," said the man as we hiked up the front steps. "I'm Stan Cunningham."

If he were fifteen years younger, he'd be the kind of man you see all the time on the cover of *GQ* magazine—good looking, intelligent, physically fit, well dressed, better-than-average teeth. Mr. Cunningham looked successful.

He gave us a big smile, but it was the kind of smile car salesmen give anybody who walks onto the lot. "Henry said you two were still in the car, so I said we ought to invite you in."

Mr. Cunningham looked at me closely. "Isn't Carl Jenkins your father?"

I really love it when people ask me questions they know the answers to. I nodded.

"I played in the Mulligan tournament with him at the country club last summer. He never said anything about having an Indian boy living with you."

"Must have slipped his mind," I said. This sort of thing happens to me when I'm nervous. I sound like I'm mouthing off even when I don't mean to. Besides, I didn't like the way Mr. Cunningham said *Indian boy* —like Henry was an artifact on loan from the Smithsonian.

Mr. Cunningham showed us inside. A black terrier with a plaid collar rushed forward and began barking noisily.

"Mom," Celia said to a woman sitting in a nearby chair, "make him stop, please."

Celia and Henry were sitting together on the couch. Celia was wearing a silky lavender dress that fit like a glove, and her light hair was pulled off her face. She definitely looked older than sixteen. Henry was tugging at his tie a little, the way he always does when he's uncomfortable. I suddenly noticed someone was wearing too much after-shave. Me.

The dog kept barking.

"Now, be a good sport and stop barking, Angus," said Celia's mother. I just love the way some people think if they stand there and reason with a dog that it will eventually see their point of view.

Angus kept right on barking.

"It's okay," Diana said. She stooped down to let Angus sniff her hand. "He'll stop once he gets used to us."

"Mo-ther," said Celia. Her cheeks were pink flames.

Mrs. Cunningham got up from her chair, picked up Angus, and disappeared down a hallway. Mr. Cunningham pulled out chairs for Diana and me.

I sat down and looked around the living room. It reminded me of the lobby of an expensive hotel.

Mr. Cunningham gave us all an easy smile that didn't quite reach his eyes.

"Celia didn't tell us very much about you," he said to Henry.

"You never *asked* me anything, Dad." Celia's voice was sweet, but you could feel its edge. She draped her hand across Henry's thigh, then stared straight at her father.

The room temperature suddenly shot up by a couple hundred degrees and I shifted my weight, wishing like crazy that we were already at China Village ordering pu-pu platters.

Mr. Cunningham leaned back in his chair and folded his arms across his chest like he was in charge of the world. Celia was still trying to catch his eyes, but he didn't notice.

I remembered what Celia had said about her dad—how strict he was, how he'd ground her forever if he ever caught her driving the car. Maybe those things were true. But now I got the distinct impression that Mr. Cunningham didn't care all that much what Celia did.

He smiled again at Henry. "Where are you from originally?"

"Arizona."

"Navaho?"

Henry nodded.

"Speak any?"

"Sure. Of course." He rubbed the palm of his hand on his pant leg.

"Why don't you say something for us?"

Henry tugged his tie again. Celia moved even closer to him.

"Dad . . ."

Mr. Cunningham ignored Celia.

"Hataali." The word came from the back of Henry's throat. "It means 'singer.' What you would call a medicine man."

Mr. Cunningham looked at Henry with the first real interest he'd shown all night. Then he smiled a little. "Do *you* believe in medicine men?"

Henry took a very deep breath but didn't answer.

Mrs. Cunningham walked back into the room. "Well!" she said, smiling brightly. "Well!"

"MY DAD CAN BE SUCH A JERK," said Celia as we drove to China Village. She tossed her head, then moved closer to Henry, who put his free arm around her.

"Why doesn't she just go ahead and sit in his lap?" Diana whispered. Henry gave her a warning glance in the rearview mirror.

I'd been thinking about holding Diana's hand, but her comment scared me off.

When we passed the parking lot of Albertson's grocery store, Diana let out a yelp, then grabbed Henry's shoulder. The car swerved and Henry swore. "Do you want to get us killed?"

"Stop the car! There's a dog tied to a lamppost!"

"There isn't time for that now, Diana." Henry spoke through tight lips.

"Stop this car *now.*"

"No." Henry's lips were getting even tighter. "We

don't have time." He punched the accelerator and Diana looked at the back of his head in disbelief.

"Fine. Then just let that dog be on your conscience!"

Celia burst out laughing, then stopped as soon as she realized no one was joining her. "I'm sorry." She turned around to look at Diana. "I really didn't mean to be rude."

I wanted to put my arm around Diana and pull her close to me. I wanted to protect her from the sound of Celia's laugh.

Henry glared at Diana again in the rearview mirror and Diana glared back.

By the time we reached China Village, I was wondering how much more *fun* things could get.

As soon as we walked through the door of the restaurant I could see that Celia was busy checking everything out—the tacky strands of plastic Chinese lanterns, the vases filled with fake flowers, the red Naugahyde booths, the moose head on the wall.

She gave a light laugh. "I see what you mean, Henry. What great decor!"

"Hey, only the very *finest* for you, Celia," I said. Something about the way my voice sounded caught Celia's attention. We looked straight at each other and the light went on in her beautiful eyes.

She understood that I was not her friend. A slow flush crawled up her cheeks. My face started to turn red too.

Nobody said much during dinner, and by the time

we finished I could tell Henry was ready to strangle a) Diana, b) me, or c) all of the above.

The waiter finally brought the check. Diana picked it up and started dividing it into four.

"What are you doing?" Henry asked. Any minute now and the veins in his neck were going to burst.

"I'm figuring out what each of us owes."

"Marcus and I will take care of it. Give me the check, *please.*"

"There's no reason why Celia and I shouldn't help."

Celia looked surprised, but she nodded. Henry turned to me for help.

"You can pay next time." I said.

"Here," said Celia, taking the check out of Diana's hand, "let me take care of it. I'd really like to." She dug deep into her purse.

Diana was about to protest, but Henry shot her such a lethal look that she slumped back in her chair instead.

"Thanks a lot, Celia," I said. My voice was full of frost.

HENRY LAID INTO ME in the men's room once we got to the school.

"What was going on between you and Celia at the restaurant?" He was shaking his hands dry and flipping beads of water all over me.

"I don't like her, Henry. Okay?"

Henry stared at me like I was crazy. "Admit it, Marcus. China Village was a lousy idea."

"Oh, yeah?" I said to him as he left the bathroom. "Well, screw you, pal." I turned the water on full blast. It splashed all over my suit.

I looked at myself in the mirror. "Oh, this is great," I said out loud. "Just great." I looked around for paper towels even though the only thing rarer than a paper towel in the men's room at our school is a girl.

"Wonderful," I said. "Terrific!" I flapped my tie around for a little while, trying to dry it off in the breeze. Two guys walked into the bathroom and gave me a funny look when they saw me waving my tie around like it was a flag. Finally I left, praying that Diana wasn't the kind of girl who noticed lots of large water stains on a person's tie.

Diana squinted when she saw me. "How'd you get all wet?"

I gave her the same pained smile I always give my dentist when he says he wants to do a little drilling. "It's a long and boring story," I said. "How about some punch?"

We walked to the punch table at the side of the gym and helped ourselves.

"I didn't mean for Celia to pay for the whole thing tonight," Diana said. She bit her lower lip.

"Forget Celia."

The band started to play a new song, a slow number this time. Out on the dance floor couples wrapped around one another. I saw Celia and Henry. Something about the way their bodies touched and swayed told me more about how they spent their time than Henry ever had.

I started wondering a little about Diana and me—if people would ever think the same thing about us. I looked at her sideways. Her hair was so beautiful. I wanted to touch it.

There was an ache inside my chest.

"Diana?"

"Hmmm?" She was watching Henry and Celia too.

"Look at me, Diana."

She turned and stared at me.

"I like it when you look at me. You have pretty eyes."

Diana just kept looking at me. I took her hand and traced one of my fingers lightly across her palm. "Please dance with me," I said.

I tightened my grip on her hand and led her to the floor, then wrapped my arms around her. The skin of her face and shoulders was smooth and warm, and her hair smelled sweet.

I guess I should have been happy then with my arms around Diana like that. But the truth is I felt lonelier than I've ever felt in my entire life. It's a strange feeling—feeling all alone in a crowd of people.

One of the band members picked up a microphone and started singing sad words that went straight inside of me. I touched Diana's hair. Maybe it was just my imagination, but I thought I felt her relax a little against me then. The music hummed through the speakers on the floor, swirling up and surrounding us.

I love you, Diana, I thought to myself. *I wish you loved me too.*

13

I DIDN'T KISS DIANA AFTER THE DANCE.

I wanted to. More than anything else in the world I wanted to. And when she let me hold her hand on the way home, I thought I'd have the guts to try. But I totally lost my nerve while I walked her to her front door. For one thing, my heart was pounding loud enough for the entire Western Hemisphere to hear. For another thing, Diana immediately grabbed the doorknob, which is always a very good sign that a girl doesn't want to be kissed. She glanced at me, then looked down at her feet.

"Thanks, Marcus. I had a great time," she said, her cheeks turning pink. Then she ran straight into the house.

Kissing. My favorite noncontact sport.

WE WEREN'T THE WORLD'S JOLLIEST CREW on the way to school Monday morning. The hearse was appropriate, since it felt exactly like we were on our way to a funeral. Even Julia noticed. "You guys sure have been acting *weird* lately," she said when we dropped her off in front of Hawthorne Elementary. She scrunched her face all up when she said the word *weird*.

Diana was the first to break the silence. "I've thought about this all weekend, Henry, and I've decided to tell you what I think—even though you won't like it."

Henry acted like he hadn't heard her. She kept talking anyway.

"I think Celia's using you."

Henry gave a short laugh. "Oh, *right*."

Diana started to turn a little pink, but she kept at him. "I saw the way she acted in front of her father, Henry. I think she's using you to get his attention."

"Why don't you give her a little more credit than that, Diana. Why don't you give *me* a little more credit than that." Henry said it so quietly that I was suddenly afraid for Diana. The quieter Henry gets, the angrier he is.

"I'm not saying she doesn't like you for yourself too." Diana was getting flustered now.

"Mind your own business, Diana," Henry hissed. "It seems to me you've got problems of your own."

I caught my breath. This was the closest any of us had come to the subject of DeeDee and the way she manages her life.

Diana looked like she'd been slapped.

I swore. "That isn't fair, Henry."

"Fair?" Henry said. "In case you haven't noticed yet, *life* isn't fair."

He punched the accelerator hard with his foot.

∘ ∘ ∘

I AVOIDED HENRY during track practice—which was pretty easy to do, since Henry was busy avoiding me too. All of us on the team were working hard, getting ready for Saturday's meet. Henry would be running for the first time since his injury. I was working on some things that Donahue had suggested to me after my last race. I had been improving slowly but surely and everyone had noticed. Except for Henry and Frank. Henry was too caught up in Frank to notice anybody else and Frank didn't notice anybody at all. He ran apart from the rest of us, his long black hair flying in the wind behind him.

By the end of the day, though, I couldn't keep my mouth shut any longer. The more I thought about the way Henry had treated Diana, the madder I got.

I found Henry upstairs in our bedroom. He was sitting at the desk working on the essay to send to New York.

"This topic really stinks," Henry said when I walked into our room. " 'The Me Nobody Knows.' Didn't it occur to those people that some of us would like to keep it that way?"

"I wanna talk to you, Henry." My voice was quiet.

"Not now."

"Now."

Henry swiveled around in the chair to face me. He looked like a little kid who was mad about the scolding he knew he was going to get.

"I just want to know"—I paused for a minute—"I

just want to know what's been going on with you lately."

Henry snorted. Then he spread his arms and shrugged. "Nothing. Nothing is going on with me except that I'm trying to finish this very boring essay."

"What you said to Diana in the hearse this morning was just plain mean. I never thought you were mean before, Henry."

"And what about the things Diana said to me?" He shot back.

"That was different and you know it," I said as evenly as I could. "You know how Diana is. That's her way of showing she really cares for you."

My heart jumped a little. I wished Diana cared for me. Not like a friend.

Henry looked at me. Then he turned back toward the desk and picked up his pen. "Get off my case."

He tried writing some more, then he threw the pen against the desktop and picked up the paper. He crumpled it into a little ball and threw it. He missed the garbage can and made Lazarus jump.

Something about the way Henry thought he could —I don't know—just dismiss me like that made me so mad that I could feel it in my head. The blood rushed to my face and eyes and for just a second the lights in the room seemed to dim.

"I think"—and now there was nothing weak or unsure about my voice—"there's a problem with the way you've been treating people lately. I can understand you not liking Frank much. But I don't understand why you have to treat Diana like she doesn't count. Or me, for that matter."

Something very strange happened inside of me when I said that. It was like a dam breaking, a dam full of resentment I had never known was there.

"You don't understand," Henry said. "You don't understand a damn thing."

My voice was very cool. "That's what everybody thinks—Fritz, Miss Brett, even you, Henry. You all say to yourself, there's good old Marcus, sitting like a bump on a log, too stupid to understand a thing. Well, you're wrong. I understand plenty."

I understood that I was tired of everybody acting like what I said and what I thought didn't count for very much at all. But how could I blame them when all I'd ever done was sleepwalk through my own life? How could I expect other people to respect me when I'd been too lazy to show any real respect for myself?

I remembered what Henry had said after he watched Frank run his first race: "I'm going to beat him, Marcus." My eyes narrowed.

I'm going to beat you, Henry. I'm going to beat you.

I'D LIKE TO SAY the day of the big race dawned bright and clear just like they always say in books. But it was raining outside. Besides, it wasn't that big of a race. Just another ordinary meet. It only felt like a big race to me. To Henry too.

I heard the rain before I opened my eyes. I could hear it ping against the window. I imagined it hitting the last of the snow, turning it to mush. I opened my eyes.

Henry was already on the floor, stretching out. His face was set in a hard, determined mask.

Henry and I said as little as possible to each other while we were getting ready. I think Mom knew something was wrong, because she kept looking at us hard. But she didn't ask questions except where she should park at the meet.

Neither of us was hungry. I could tell Henry was forcing himself to tank up on sausage and pancakes— just like me. By the time we got ready to leave, it had stopped raining.

"See you later," Dad said, browsing through the Saturday-morning paper, looking for the write-up about last night's Jazz game. "We'll all be there in time for your race."

"Diana too!" Mom called after us. "She's coming with us. Good luck!"

When Henry and I got to school, I saw him scan the field. But Frank buddy wasn't around.

"Maybe he won't show," I said, reading Henry's mind. I was amazed I could still do it.

Henry looked startled too. Then the surprise left and I couldn't see anything at all play across his face.

"I don't care what Frank does," said Henry as he turned to walk toward the locker room.

I watched him go. "Whatever you say, pal."

FRANK SHOWED UP by the time our race was called and a pack of us stepped onto the track. I knew

Henry saw him and nobody else. I didn't even exist. *That's how little of a threat you are.* The back of my neck burned with anger.

I looked at Frank. He threw back his head and shook out his hair. I doubted he saw anybody. Frank— he was as cool as winter. You know how some people are born with something missing—fingers, toes, whatever? Well, Frank was born without nerves.

I was so worked up, I was panting—and the race hadn't even started.

"Runners, take your mark," the voice boomed over the loudspeaker. We settled into our stances. I looked down the stretch of track. Then I tucked my head, took a deep breath, pulled in my thoughts, and waited for the sound of the gun.

Crack!

The pack began to move like one big animal with lots of arms and legs. After half a lap the pack began thinning into individual runners.

I was running a good race. I'd gotten off to a fast start without burning myself out. I felt it all coming together for me—my breathing, my motion, my mind. I kept at it.

With only one lap left, three of us were way ahead, running together in a small tight pack. Henry first. Frank second. Me third.

We had half a lap left. I could feel Frank start to make his move on Henry. I moved to keep up with Frank. As soon as I did, I knew that I had nothing left. I could hang on to third, but that was all.

Henry had felt Frank's move, too, and he was pulling away. But Frank stayed with him, matching him step for step, stride for stride, the two of them stretching for the tape just ahead.

Closer, closer—then Frank pulled the race out from underneath Henry's feet, like a rug. One last incredible burst and he broke the tape.

Henry followed Frank over the finish line, then lost his stride and tumbled to the ground. He lay on the track in a heap of knees and elbows. I nearly fell on top of him. The rest of the runners had to bob and weave to miss him.

I thought he might have hurt his ankle again, but he was back on his feet before anyone had a chance to help him up.

Frank was bent over, trying to catch his breath. When he looked up, he saw Henry. "In your face." He mouthed the words so Henry could see them, and then he gave Henry an ugly smile.

"Son of a bitch!" Henry shouted. He ran for Frank, grabbed him around the neck, threw him to the ground. Henry was on him in a flash.

"No!" I grabbed his shoulders and tried to pull him off Frank. "Don't be stupid. It's not worth it!"

I heard Coach Donahue and some of the others yelling, trying to break up the fight.

Henry shook me off his back. Then he stood up, spun around, and planted his fist in my face. Light exploded inside my head. My teeth, my eyes, my cheekbones, the insides of my ears, rang with pain. I could feel the blood spurt from my nose.

Without thinking I swung back. Hard.

Someone grabbed me from behind. Coach Donahue had Henry in a neck hold. One of the other guys was helping up Frank, who looked dazed.

"What the hell is going on here?" Donahue yelled.

Henry's eyes found mine. The wildness slipped from his face.

"Marcus . . ." He tried to move toward me, but Donahue held him tight.

I shook myself free and stepped back.

"Don't," I said in a low voice. "Don't you touch me."

Then I turned and walked toward the locker room. I could feel the blood run over my mouth, down my chin. People stepped aside and let me pass.

"*Marcus!*" I could hear Henry shouting after me. "*Marcus—*"

No one else was in the locker room. I found a clean towel and soaked it in cold water. I lay down on a bench and wished for just a minute that I was dead. Then I covered my face with the towel.

That way if someone came in, they'd never know I was crying.

ONCE MY NOSE STOPPED BLEEDING, I grabbed my gear and left. I didn't bother to shower and change, even though the front of my shirt was stiff with blood. I didn't care if I got in trouble for leaving.

Everyone was still at the track meet when I got home. Was Diana with them? Maybe she'd seen what had happened too. I started feeling pretty stupid then. That's always how it works once you cool down. You start realizing what a first-class idiot you've made of yourself.

I ran upstairs to my room. I slammed the door shut and flopped onto the bed. I could hardly breathe, my face hurt so bad.

Fifteen minutes or so went by. I heard Dad's Chevy pull up in the driveway. A minute or two later I heard the front door open and shut. I waited for Julia to scream up the stairway to me, but she didn't. Everyone was downstairs being real quiet.

Finally there was a knock on my door.

"Marcus?" It was Dad. "Can I come in?"

"Okay."

The door opened a crack, then wider. He came in and sat on the edge of my bed. "You look terrible."

"Thanks."

Dad touched my nose. I quickly sucked in air through my mouth.

"Shit, Dad!"

He just kept feeling my nose and saying, "Hmm." It's a good thing he decided to become a psychiatrist instead of a brain surgeon. The guy does not have the world's lightest touch.

"We need to get you to the hospital right now." His glasses were slipping down his nose, but he didn't even bother to push them back into place. "I think your nose is broken again."

"Swell."

Since I hold Lake View's Babe Ruth League record for taking fastballs in the face, I happen to know that having a broken nose fixed is one of life's more unpleasant experiences. For one thing, the doctor puts so many needles up your nose to deaden it that you start feeling like your face is a stinking pincushion. Then he resets it. He says you won't feel a thing, but I always do. Maybe because I'm such a sensitive guy.

"Let's go," said Dad, giving me a hand.

Mom and Julia were downstairs in the kitchen. For once in her life Julia didn't say anything. She just stared at me with wide round eyes. Mom kissed me on the cheek. "Love you, Marcus."

Dad and I drove in silence to the hospital. He didn't even turn on the radio. I could hear the wind outside. I used to like the wind when I was a little kid, the way it blew my hair straight up on end and made my nose go cold. But lately the sound of wind made me think of empty places—burned-over fields and broken-down houses where nobody lived anymore.

"Are you going to be okay?" Dad finally asked.

"Fine. I love looking like this. It drives all the girls wild."

"I'm not talking about your nose."

I didn't say anything.

"I just want to know if you're going to be okay." Dad changed his grip on the steering wheel.

I looked outside. "Henry's changed, Dad. I don't know him anymore." My nose was killing me. In fact, I was sore all over. I wanted a new nose. I wanted a new body. I wanted a new life.

Dad thought for a minute. "You've changed too."

"Yeah, right."

"That was one hell of race you ran this morning."

With everything that had happened, I'd completely forgotten that I'd placed just behind two of the fastest runners around.

"I don't even know my time."

"I do," said Dad. "Your mother and I checked before coming home."

I whistled when he told me.

"Pretty slick," Dad agreed. "I wonder what the difference was?"

I looked at him, my face a big swollen blank.

"The Marcus I knew six months ago didn't have it in him to run a race like that."

Then he flipped on the radio, filling the car with the drone of a country guitar.

14

HENRY HADN'T COME HOME.

Day stretched into early evening, and Henry still wasn't home. I could hear Mom and Dad talking about him in the kitchen. Only, they weren't just talking—they were arguing.

"I think we ought to go look for him right now." Mom was trying to keep her voice down, since Julia was in the kitchen too. "He needs to be with us."

"He needs to be alone," Dad said.

"How do *you* know?"

Dad didn't answer.

"Oh, I forgot," Mom said. "You know *everything*. Just like Mr. Wizard."

It doesn't bug Dad if I accuse him of being a know-it-all, but he goes a little nuts whenever my mom does. "Look, Betsy," he exploded, "Henry needs some distance from us right now. I'm afraid we're a part of the problem."

Mom snorted.

"When I saw him take after that kid today, a light went on inside my head. God knows how much I love

Henry, but maybe Lennie was wrong to ever send him here. Maybe we were wrong to let him live with us—"

"That's ridiculous, and you know it," Mom said so coldly, you'd almost think her lips were turning blue with frostbite.

I looked at myself in the hallway mirror. The skin beneath my eyes was turning a puffy purple, and my nose looked like a small water balloon. At least the doctor hadn't bandaged me. The last time I broke my nose he'd made me wear a fiberglass mask that made me look like Spider-Man. I once wrote an essay about the experience called "My Life as a Junior High Freak Show."

The telephone rang. Mom picked it up.

"Yes," I heard her say. "Henry lives with us."

I drifted toward the kitchen just in time to see the color drain from Mom's face. She picked up a pen and started scribbling stuff all over a yellow legal pad while saying, "Uh-hum," into the receiver.

"What's the matter, Mom?" Julia whispered loudly. "What is it?"

She hung up the phone and looked straight at Dad. "Henry's father . . ." she said in a tiny voice that didn't sound like her own at all, "he's been shot."

"Oh, no," Dad said. Julia's eyes were huge.

"He's okay, though, isn't he?" I couldn't believe it. Only people on TV got shot.

"He's really hurt," Mom said quietly.

Tears jumped to Julia's eyes. "This is awful!" she wailed. "Oh, poor Henry—poor Lennie!"

Suddenly I felt like I was watching and hearing things in a movie.

"What happened?" Dad was asking Mom.

"Lennie got word that there was a loud drinking party going on, so he and a partner went to investigate. When they were walking up to the house, someone saw them and took a shot out of the window. The bullet hit him. He's alive, but he's in critical condition."

Mom moved across the room and folded me in her arms. Then she pulled away and looked at me. "Find him," she whispered fiercely.

Outside, the day had turned perfect. Just when everything starts to fall apart, the weather decides to get gorgeous.

For a split second I thought about taking Diana with me. But I had to find Henry, and I had to be alone when I found him.

Where to go?

I tried to think of his usual hangouts. The library. The theater. The park. The mall. The canyon. The lake. I was missing something. Something obvious. I knew I was, but I couldn't think of what it was.

Then it struck me. He would have gone to Celia's.

I drove over in the hearse and pulled up the long steep driveway. I flew out of the car and rang the doorbell. I could hear Angus barking. I rang the doorbell again. Angus kept barking.

"Quiet!" I heard Celia say, and then she opened the door.

Her eyes were red and swollen, and the skin beneath them was smeared with black. My stomach took a dive because I was afraid she might cry some more in front of me, and I wouldn't know what to do.

"What do you want, Marcus?" she asked, looking at my face.

"Is Henry here?"

She gave a short laugh. "Well, he *was* here."

I stood there on her front porch shivering, even though it wasn't cold. "I have to find him, Celia. Did he say where he was going?"

She looked at me, her eyes practically shooting me. "Henry wouldn't tell me something as important as *that*." She bit off the end of every single word. "I don't mean jack to him, Marcus."

I stared at her like she was crazy.

"Look, why don't you come inside for a minute." Celia pushed the door open for me.

"He came here after the meet," she said as I followed her through the living room and into the kitchen. "I didn't go because I was trying to finish this to show him how much I care." Celia pointed to a painting on an easel standing in the corner.

It was Henry's portrait.

"I paint in here whenever my parents go out of town because the light is so good." Celia's words were like the songs you hear over the telephone when someone puts you on hold—I barely noticed them. I was too busy looking at the painting.

It showed Henry sitting on a stool by a window streaming with blue and yellow light. He was wearing a white cotton T-shirt and faded jeans—just like always. The pose was exactly right too. Head cocked slightly to the right, shoulders slumped a little forward, arms loosely folded.

But the face. The face was wrong.

Henry's low forehead and slanted eyes, his broad sculpted cheeks and wide straight nose, his square jaw and thin molded lips, had all been softened. He looked like a white person painted brown.

"I showed it to Henry when he came," Celia said, her voice trembling. "You know what he did? He stared at it for a long time without saying a word. Then he started to laugh. He *laughed* at it. At me."

I could hear the ghost of Henry's laughter still. Soft. Piercing. Unforgiving. He'd seen what I had seen.

I glanced up at Celia. Even with swollen eyes and hair hanging in her face, she was still beautiful. And that was all I really knew about her.

I remembered what Henry had said to Diana in the lunchroom—that other girls automatically hate someone like Celia because they're threatened by her looks. Even Diana, who's the fairest person I know, didn't give Celia a chance. But guys are just as bad. They see someone who looks like Celia, and they don't even take the time to find out who she really is.

I caught Celia's eyes.

"What happened to your face?" she asked.

"Henry decked me."

Tears jumped to her eyes. "I'm so sorry."

"I'm the one who's sorry, Celia. I was a real jerk to you the night of the dance. You didn't deserve it."

She stared at me. "What?"

I buried my hands in my pockets. "I gotta go now."

"Marcus, wait. Thanks." She smiled at me a little. "But listen. When you see Henry, tell him something for me—tell him to go to hell."

Her eyes were wet and bright.

I ran back to the hearse. I *had* to find Henry. And when I did, I had to tell him about Lennie.

I drove all over town, hardly noticing the lights changing from green to red to green again. And then I thought about all those nights when he used to go out and run by himself.

I headed toward the school. When I got there I parked the car and ran toward the track. Every step I took made my face throb. I swallowed hard to keep from throwing up.

Henry was on the far side of the track, running. I took a seat on the front row of the bleachers and watched him. It had been a long time since I'd actually watched Henry run. Usually I was running with him—or against him.

How can I describe how Henry looks when he runs? He looks more animal than human. Something totally strong and sleek and sure of itself. A greyhound. A cheetah. A hawk wheeling across a ceiling of sky.

My throat went tight.

Henry finally saw me. He slowed his pace and then stopped in front of the bleachers. He bent over, put his hands on his knees, and tried to catch his breath.

"Henry."

He looked at me, his black eyes filled with the pain of running, the pain of thinking. "Look at you!" He stepped closer, then sat down. "I'm sorry."

"Forget it."

"I never thought I could do something like that to you." He shut his eyes tight. "How do you feel?"

"It doesn't matter." And it didn't. Nothing mattered right now except Lennie.

"Like hell it doesn't matter!" His voice cracked. "Marcus—"

"Wait. I have to tell you something."

For an instant the two of us sat still as statues listening to the noises of the night—cars, birds, a train somewhere in the distance. All these years, I thought. All these years I'd leaned on Henry to carry me through. And now, for a little while at least, Henry would have to lean on me. I took a long, deep breath.

"Your father, Henry," I told him softly. "He's been hurt. Bad."

15

HENRY LEFT THE NEXT DAY.

Dad and I drove him to the depot. None of us said much. Dad reached into his cassette case and flipped a Waylon Jennings tape into the tape deck.

Henry started to smile. "I'll be getting a bellyful of CW where I'm going." Then he looked out the window.

When we got to the bus depot, Dad took out a hundred-dollar bill and tried to give it to him.

"I'm not taking it," Henry said.

Dad looked at Henry squarely. "It's not for you. Use it for your grandfather. Buy him a few new shirts. Help him with groceries. It would mean a lot to him if his grandson did that for him. Pay me back later."

Henry looked at Dad, then took the money. "I will," he said. "I will pay you back."

"I know." Dad took Henry and hugged him hard, just as if Henry was a little kid all over again. Henry wrapped his arms around Dad.

"Thanks, Boss," he said in a low voice, "for everything."

"When do you think he'll be back?" I asked as we drove home.

But Dad just looked straight out the windshield and kept on driving as if he hadn't heard.

HENRY HAD BEEN GONE FOR A WEEK. He called twice with the news that his dad was doing better than they thought he would.

Diana and I were eating lunch together at school, and I was thinking about how strange things had been between us ever since the evening of the school dance. Sometimes, like when we were on our way to school, I could feel her looking at me. If I happened to catch her eye, she'd turn bright red. Occasionally she'd be saying something to me, then lose her train of thought right in the middle of her sentence.

I knew what the problem was. She knew I had a thing for her, and that changed everything. Now I made her uncomfortable. I was beginning to wish that I'd never invited her to the dance. Then things would have been the same as they always had been between us. Except for the fact that I had a hard time breathing when I was around her.

Today, though, there was something other than the fact that I made Diana nervous. She was really upset about something.

"What's the matter?" I finally asked, wishing for the hundredth time that my face didn't look like raw hamburger.

She was picking at her food, which is something she usually doesn't do.

"Come on," I said. "You can tell me. I take how-to-listen lessons from Dad."

She put down her fork and looked at me.

"It's my new stepfather-to-be."

"Thom with an *h*?"

"He doesn't like animals, Marcus. My mother says I have to get rid of Boston. It's *always* like this. She totally rearranges everything in our lives for her new man. She changes everything except for the one thing that ends up driving all of them away."

"She wants you to get rid of Boston?" I couldn't believe DeeDee would do something like that. Then I had an idea.

"Hey! It's no problem. I'll take Boston. Yeah! I'll take him. He can live at my house. I can see it now. Boston and I will be like this"—I crossed two of my fingers. "Boston and I will be bloods."

Diana looked at me and then she smiled. She even laughed. I like the sound of Diana's laugh because it always sounds real. She laughs because she wants to, not because she's supposed to.

She grew serious again. "Actually, this has forced me to make a decision I should have made before. I stopped thinking clearly about Boston a long time ago. I stopped thinking about what was best for him and started thinking only about what was best for me. Boston's in terrible pain, but I just didn't want to see that. I'm going to take him to the vet this afternoon and have him put to sleep."

I didn't know what to say except "I'm sorry."

"Can you do me a favor?"

Anything, I told her in my mind. *Anything at all.*

Diana blushed, and for a minute I thought I'd spoken out loud. "Sure," I told her evenly. "What do you need?"

"Will you drive me and Boston to the vet's office this afternoon? My mother said she'd take me, but I don't want her near me."

"I'd be happy to take you."

I told Donahue I'd be missing practice that afternoon. Then I drove Diana home from school and went inside with her. As I walked through the front door, it occurred to me that I hadn't been in Diana's house that many times. When DeeDee or Diana wanted to talk, they usually came to our house.

DeeDee was sitting in the living room, thumbing through some fashion magazine.

"God, Marcus, look at *this* horrible outfit!" She laughed deep inside her throat, then held up the magazine so I could see. Picking out ugly clothes in magazines is one of DeeDee's favorite games.

DeeDee, on the other hand, was looking pretty good in her new pink sweatsuit. She has great taste in clothes—which is a good thing, since she spends a lot of money on them. Sometimes she even buys outfits for Julia, which really embarrasses my mother.

I sat down in the leather wing chair by the front window and looked outside.

DeeDee rustled through the magazine for a few more minutes, then put it down. "Marcus?"

I looked at her.

She lifted an eyebrow, then drawled like she was

from the South. "Are you mad at me, too, honey?" DeeDee does accents.

Her question made me squirm. Did she really want me to tell her the truth?

DeeDee dropped her magazine so that it landed open with a little *plop* on the floor. Diana would never toss anything aside like that—she takes care of everything.

DeeDee got out of her chair and walked over to the window near my chair. "We've been friends for a long time. Please don't be mad at me." She'd dropped the accent. "I hate it when people get mad at me. *I* feel bad about Boston too."

Did she think she deserved points for that?

Diana came down the stairs with Boston following her. I got up from my chair. Diana put a leash on him as soon as he finished hobbling down the stairs.

DeeDee went over to Diana, and something about her expression surprised me a little. She looked like she was *afraid* of her own daughter. DeeDee gave her a little hug. Diana didn't move a muscle and the look she gave DeeDee could have turned her to ice. She went out the front door with Boston.

DeeDee looked at me and whispered, "Thank you, Marcus." She turned to go.

"Why are you doing this to Diana?" I burst out. She looked back at me with wide blue eyes. "Can't you see what you're doing to her?"

"We talked about it and she agreed that this is the best thing," DeeDee faltered. "She's doing this for Boston."

"That's very true. But she's also doing it because *you* told her to do something about Boston!" I shouted at her. I could feel my heart beating in my throat.

DeeDee looked like she'd been hit.

"Why don't you give Diana a break and try being the grown-up for a change?" Then I left her standing alone by the stairway.

BOSTON sat between Diana and me on the front seat of the hearse. He had his head in Diana's lap. Every now and then he'd pick up his head and look at me with that funny puzzled look all boxers have.

"Hey, buddy," I said.

Diana stroked his head.

The linoleum floors in the vet's waiting room were clean and the magazines were stacked neatly in a rack on the north wall. But it was a depressing place. Maybe it only felt that way to me because I knew why we had come.

"Can I help you?" asked the receptionist.

"Yes," said Diana. "I called earlier. I'll—I'll be having my dog put to sleep this afternoon."

The woman gave Diana and Boston a sympathetic look.

"Would you like to leave him here?"

"Oh, no!" Diana said. "I want to be with him when he goes."

"That will be just fine," the woman said gently. "You can hold him in your arms. He won't feel a thing, but it will comfort him to have you there."

It all sounded pretty grim to me. "You don't really want to stay, do you?"

"Of course I do!"

I could tell just by looking at her face that arguing wouldn't be any use.

I let out a sigh. "Whatever you want."

I took a seat. Diana filled out a few papers, then joined me.

Boston was shaking. He kept looking at Diana, but he didn't bark or whine. Diana was silent and white.

The receptionist disappeared, then came back.

"The doctor will see you now, dear."

I looked at Diana and swallowed hard. "You want me to go with you?"

I hoped she sould say no.

"No. Wait here."

I waited for a long, long time.

When Diana returned to the waiting room, she was holding Boston's collar and leash in one hand. Her eyes were red but she wasn't crying. The vet, Dr. Douglas, followed her out.

"No charge for this one, Myrt," he told the receptionist.

Diana looked surprised.

"You know who this is, don't you? This is the girl who organized the animal rescue team down at the high school."

Myrt gave Diana a warm smile. "A celebrity!"

Diana smiled a little. "Not really," she said, but I could tell she was pleased.

Dr. Douglas took Diana's hand and shook it. "This

may be very premature of me, but if I ever run into a nice litter of boxers, shall I call you?"

Diana started to shake her head no, then she stopped. "That would be very nice."

"I thought Thom with an *h* was allergic to dogs," I said when we went outside together.

"He is. But Thom won't be around forever." She paused. Then she said quietly, "And neither will I."

We got in the car and started home.

"Would you mind if we drove around for a little while?" Diana asked.

"Sounds okay to me."

We drove all over the place—through town, down by the lake, along the road past the high school. I remembered how Diana had looked that night when she disappeared singing into the fog.

"Thanks for being so nice today," she said.

"Don't tell anybody. I don't want people to know what a great guy I really am."

She laughed. Then she stopped, and her face turned red. I'd never thought of Diana as a blusher, but it seemed like every time I turned around these days she was changing colors.

"I want to tell you something, Marcus. Don't think I'm stupid."

"I won't think you're stupid."

"I think—I don't know. . . ."

"Beating around the bush isn't exactly your style, Diana. Out with it."

"I think I might—love you."

Everything inside of me started singing a little song. *Diana loves you. Diana loves you.* But I played it completely cool on the outside.

"Well, I don't blame you."

Diana's mouth fell open, and I grinned.

"Come here," I said. She paused, then slid next to me. I put my arm around her shoulders. It fit there perfectly, just like I knew it would.

We drove up the canyon until we came to an empty campground. I turned off the engine, then pulled Diana close to me. I could hear the wind whispering through the tops of the trees.

"I love you too," I told her quietly.

She slipped her arms around my neck and looked straight into my eyes. Then she kissed me, accidentally bumping my nose as she did. I practically flew out the window.

"Oh, your poor nose!" Diana turned red.

We looked at each other, then burst out laughing. A strand of loose hair tumbled across her forehead, and I pushed it gently out of her face.

I kissed the little smile on her lips.

THAT NIGHT WHEN I WENT TO WORK, Fritz yelled at me.

"Gomer!"

I looked at Fritz, straightened my cardboard collar, and said, "My name isn't Gomer. It isn't pinhead, soldier boy, or geek. It's Marcus to you. *Comprendo?*"

Fritz just stared at me.

"Hey, what's gotten into you? Come back here!" he screamed after me as I left his office and took my station behind the concession counter. *"On the double!"*

16

UNFORTUNATELY, Diana and I didn't spend much time together while Henry was gone—thanks very much to Mr. Fritz Minster, the village idiot. He was mad at Henry for leaving town during the annual Arnold Schwarzenegger Film Festival, so naturally he took it out on me. I worked every stinking night. With Henry gone, Camelot Theater felt exactly like the inside of a tomb.

Henry was there when I got home from work Sunday night. He and my parents and Julia were sitting around the dining-room table playing the usual Sunday-night game of Scrabble. Everybody was looking and acting very normal. When I walked through the door, I could hear Julia reading the rules out loud in her schoolteacher voice.

" 'All words labeled as a part of speech (including those listed of foreign origin, and as archaic, obsolete, colloquial, slang, et cetera) are permitted with the exception of the following—' "

"Now, I want you to please listen to this, Betsy," Dad said. His face was so red, it practically glowed, and he was talking way too loud. Mom just blinked at him like an owl through her big round glasses.

"Julia doesn't need to read *me* any rules, Carl," Mom said. "You're just mad because I'm winning. Again."

"*Dillest* is *not* a word," Dad roared at her.

Henry was leaning back in his chair, arms folded across his chest, watching Mom and Dad having one of their traditional Scrabble fights.

"It's a comparative adjective, as in 'Now, isn't that the dillest pickle you've ever tasted?' " she explained.

Henry burst out laughing. The sudden noise made Lazarus shoot straight out of Henry's lap just like a bottle rocket on the Fourth of July.

I laughed too. Everyone turned around to look at me.

"Hi, honey," said Mom, looking pretty pleased with herself. "I'm stomping your father."

"She cheats!" Dad said. Mom pulled a face at him, then smiled again at me.

"*Look* at my ears, Marcus," Julia demanded.

I squinted. "They're on the sides of your head, Legs. Right where you left them."

"Quit being stupid," Julia said. Then she flipped her head from side to side like she was trying out for the high-school drill team. I noticed she had on a new pair of dangly earrings that clanked against her jaw like a matched set of wind chimes.

"Henry brought these home for me," she said.

"And he brought this for your dad and me," said Mom. She pulled something out of the paper sack by her chair. It was a blanket full of geometric designs done in black, red, and turquoise.

"Very nice," I said.

"Here. This is for you." Henry tossed me a little white sack and I opened it.

"A bolo tie, Henry?" I said, lifting it out of the sack. A bolo tie is a shoestring tie with a silver-and-turquoise clasp at the neck. You have to be at least seventy-five years old to wear one.

Everybody, including me, started to laugh. I slipped the tie around my neck. "What can I say? It's me."

For just a minute it felt like everything was just the way it always had been. I turned to Henry.

"Welcome home, Dr. Doom," I said.

I LOOKED AT THE CLOCK. It was two A.M.

I'd been awake for half an hour now. I'd been trying to go back to sleep, but I couldn't.

I went to the beach in California once when I was a kid. I still remember what the waves looked like trapped in a little sand pool Dad dug with Henry and me. The water swirled. That's what my thoughts were doing now—they kept swirling around the inside of my head, keeping me awake. I felt hot. I kicked the covers off.

"You're awake too," Henry whispered.

"Yeah."

"I can't sleep," he said.

"Me neither."

I could see the moon outside our bedroom window. It was full and bright and looked almost twice as big as it usually does. That happens here sometimes. The moon turns gold and hangs way low over the mountains just like a midnight sun.

"Let's run," said Henry suddenly.

"Now?"

I could feel Henry smile in the dark.

"Yeah. Now."

I smiled too.

We got out of bed and put on our running clothes.

"You're crazy," I told him as we slipped out the front door.

"A maniac," he agreed. Then he laughed. Just like the old Henry. "Let's run to the mouth of the canyon and back."

That would take us on the road that went past the high school. It turned into a lonely stretch of road—lined by fruit orchards and horse corrals and empty fields. It was my favorite route.

Henry and I ran at a quick but easy pace. I knew that Henry was the better runner still, and he probably always would be. But I knew that I was good too. I could run my own race and be proud of it.

"It's different in the desert than it is here," Henry was saying. "You're on top of a plateau there and the sky is so close, you almost feel like you're wearing it for a hat."

The picture of Henry wearing the sky on his head made me laugh.

It was completely quiet. There were no cars, no people. Just night. Apple trees stood in straight rows off the side of the road, like guys lined up for roll call in gym class. Not long ago their branches had been loaded with snow. Now they were covered with hard little buds getting ready to be blossoms.

"How's your dad doing?" I asked finally.

"Okay, I guess, for a guy who took a bullet."

"I guess you two spent a lot of time together," I said.

"A week isn't very much time."

"What about your grandpa? How's he doing?"

"He misses me. It sort of surprised me to realize that. I haven't been home for such a long time."

Home? I thought. *This is your home.* We ran for a while without saying anything.

"I've got a question for you," said Henry. "If somebody were to ask you what your dad's favorite sport is, what would you say?"

"Easy. Basketball."

"His favorite color?"

"Blue."

"Favorite food?"

"Mexican in general. Chile relleños in particular."

"Movie?"

"I don't know."

"Come on. Think!"

"High Noon."

Henry didn't say any more.

"So, did I pass the pop quiz?" I asked.

"Oh, yeah. You did just great. I'm the one who flunked."

"You know all that stuff about Dad too," I said.

"I know it about *your* dad. Not mine. Sitting by his bedside was like sitting by the bedside of a total stranger."

I didn't say anything.

"I ended up spending a lot of time with my grandfather. He wants to teach me things," Henry said.

"Like what?"

"He wants me to understand how Navahos like him—traditional Navahos—see the world." He paused. "Did I ever tell you about Coyote when we were kids?"

"Coyote?" I asked. "I guess you never did."

"Now, *that* surprises me. I still remember Coyote, but then he's pretty hard to forget." I could tell by the sound of Henry's voice that he was smiling a little. "Coyote is a supernatural being. He's merciful, he's cruel. He's obscene, he's holy. He gave The People fire, but he dances with witches. Coyote changes shape right before your very eyes."

I shivered in spite of myself.

"The world is full of magic for Navahos like my grandfather," said Henry. "He told me where the Diné—that's what Navahos call themselves—came from. He said they migrated upward through several different worlds layered on top of one another until they reached this world. There are stars in the spaces between the worlds. They are guides for The People."

I lifted my head and saw stars. The stars Henry's grandfather saw too.

"I don't think you ever really knew how homesick I used to get," Henry said.

"That's why you went home after you got sick."

"I was still homesick even after I came back. Remember how we used to drag our sleeping bags outside at night and lie on our backs because I wanted to look at the stars?"

I laughed a little. "Yeah, I remember. I used to look for shapes in the mountains. Rocks that looked like noses. Things like that."

Henry laughed too. And then he said, "I'd just stare and stare and stare, and before long I felt like I was floating up into the sky, that I was turning into a star too. Hard and bright and untouchable. Then I'd get scared because the feeling of floating away was so *real.* Remember how I used to run inside and stand as close as I could to the Boss? I wanted to feel safe again. Still, I always knew that if I needed a place to run to, I could run to the stars and nobody would ever know what I was doing."

Nobody, I thought. *Not even me.* It was like that night with Diana all over again. You could live forever with a person and not know things. Not until they changed shape—

"Then I stopped being homesick," Henry went on, "and some time after that I stopped feeling different. One day I even realized that I felt—I felt white inside. I knew I wasn't, but I *felt* white and that was okay with me because it made things more convenient. I don't even know how it happened. I didn't make a conscious decision to feel that way or to do whatever I had to do to fit in up here. It's just that your family always made me feel like I belonged. I love you guys, Marcus."

Whenever you run, you always hit a point when you feel like quitting. Your legs hurt, your breath is choppy. But if you can make it past that point—if you keep going—you suddenly feel like you can run forever. I felt that way now. I felt like I could run until dawn. I could run and listen until day came spilling down the mountains.

"Then Frank showed up," said Henry. "At first he just reminded me of the things I used to miss—desert sounds and smells, the feel of hot wind on my neck, things I haven't thought about for a long, long time." He paused. "Then he made me feel guilty, Marcus, like I'd sold out somehow. I'll tell you what he really did—he reminded me that I'm not white no matter how much I pretend to be, and he made me realize that I'm not Navaho either. I'm not Anglo. I'm not Navaho. I'm nothing."

Nothing! I cringed inside. "You're yourself and that's the thing that matters," I said.

Henry didn't answer.

"Look. When you talk like that you're putting skin color above everything else, Henry."

Still no answer.

"Do you think you could have done it?" he asked finally. "Left your home and your father and gone to live with strangers who didn't even look like you when you were only seven years old?"

I remembered that time in the trading post when those little Navaho kids looked at me like I was some kind of freak. I remembered how different I felt from everybody else there and how glad I was to get in the car with my dad and drive away. For a split second I felt what it must have been like for Henry when he first came to live with us. Seven years old. Scared. Different. Alone. Far away from home.

And suddenly in my mind I had an image of Henry all grown up—running at night, running away from some unknown ghost. Only, I knew what the ghost was now. I could finally give it a name. It was loneliness, a loneliness as deep as the desert itself. No matter how much Mom, Dad, Julia, and I had cared about him, in the end we hadn't been enough to make him feel whole.

Henry and I kept running. The sound of our shoes striking the road filled my ears.

Slap! Slap! Slap! Something was happening inside of me. I'd never seen Henry's loneliness. Not until tonight. And now that I had I felt—how did I feel?

Slap! Slap!

I felt betrayed. And I felt afraid.

"Marcus."

My own name sounded strange in my ears.

"Marcus," Henry said again.

"Yeah?"

"I have to tell you something."

I didn't say anything, but fear started to spread throughout my entire body.

"I'm going back to the reservation this summer."

"Why?"

"A lot of reasons," said Henry.

The fear kept right on spreading through me. *NO!* I shouted inside my head. *You can't go.*

"I want to make things right with my own father," Henry was saying. "All these years I've been mad at him for sending me away, and I never even knew it until I saw him nearly die."

Don't tell me. I don't want to hear any more.

"I want to spend more time with my grandfather. I want to learn to see, *to feel,* the world the way he does. Do you know what? The door of his hogan faces east so that the first thing he sees every morning is Father Sun. His whole life is a prayer."

"What about New York?" I tried to keep my voice as casual as possible.

"I'll have to withdraw my application."

"Miss Brett is going to throw a world-class fit."

Henry winced, but he said, "Who cares?"

"Remember what she said about having a responsibility toward your talent? She won't understand why you want to go to Arizona when you could go to New York instead." My voice no longer sounded casual. It sounded angry. Worse than that, it sounded desperate.

"I've been thinking lately that there's more than one way to develop whatever gifts I might have. When I listened to my grandfather talk about ordinary things like desert plants and animals that hunt by night, when he talked about stars and sand, I felt like I was listening to *poetry,* Marcus. I get the feeling that there are poems there, waiting for me to find them."

A cloud slipped in front of the moon. It glowed, just like the inside of a shell.

"Fine. So we don't go to New York this summer.

You'll find your poems this summer, and then you'll be back for our senior year in the fall."

"I don't know about that yet," Henry said slowly. "I don't know about anything anymore."

I stopped dead in my tracks. Henry stopped too. He turned to face me. Neither of us said anything. We just stood there in the middle of the road staring at each other. Even though it was cool outside, I was covered with sweat, and so was Henry. Both of us were breathing hard.

"I guess I just want you to tell me it's okay," said Henry, and he was pleading now, "even if you don't understand—"

"Well, you sure as hell got that one right!" I exploded. "The reservation instead of here?"

Where are you going to live, Henry Yazzie? In a trailer with your father? In a hogan with your grandfather?

"Goddammit, look at me, Marcus!" Henry shouted back, and his voice was as fierce as knives. "Look at my face! It doesn't matter what I feel like inside, I'm not white. I'm Navaho and I want to find out what that means. I want to know who I am."

I could almost see his words, hanging and shivering like dry leaves in the air between us.

I didn't say anything. I just turned and I started to run again. My arms and my legs pumped mechanically, automatically. I could hardly feel them. It was almost as though they belonged to somebody else.

I felt Henry trying to catch me. I heard his ragged breathing.

"Please, Marcus—"

You've died and gone to Fantasyland, Henry Yazzie. Let me tell you what you'll find instead of all your lovely poems. You'll find poverty. Dirt. Disease. You'll find people who hate you because of everything you've had. You'll be a hundred times more different there than you ever were here.

I threw my head back—just like Frank. Then I picked up my pace and left Henry far behind me.

17

SCHOOL WAS JUST ABOUT OVER.

The days were getting longer and warmer, and the air was filled with the smell of something blooming. Lilacs, Mom told me. I asked her, because I remembered the smell from when I was a kid and Henry and I used to stay at my grandmother's house. She had this huge lilac bush growing right next to her porch. Once when we were about eight years old, Henry and I picked all the flowers off the bush and had a big lilac fight. My grandma nearly killed us when she walked outside and found us pelting each other with all her purple flowers. It also didn't help that Henry accidentally lobbed one into the side of her head when she first stepped onto the porch.

My grandma's dead now. I haven't been back to her house since then. Maybe the old lilac bush isn't even there anymore—and I don't really want to see what the house looks like without it.

It was still light outside after Mom, Julia, Henry, and I finished eating dinner. I decided to pick up Diana and take a drive down to the lake.

"The lake?" Mom asked when I told her where I was going. "What are you going to do at the lake?"

"Oh, you know," I answered her, "appreciate nature. Stuff like that."

"Bet you're going to take Di-ana!" said Julia in her stupid little-sister singsong voice.

These days, however, I knew exactly how to handle her.

"How correct you are, Legs," I said to her. Then I put my face close to hers and stared straight into her eyeballs without blinking once. "Diana and I are going to exchange pointers"—I dropped my voice to a low growl—"on kissing."

Julia turned bright red. I stood up and started to laugh. So did Henry, who was sitting across the table from her.

"Shut up, you guys," said Julia. "Just shut up and leave me alone!" For a minute I thought she was going to stick her tongue out at us, but I think it got tangled up in her braces.

I loved it. It used to be that Julia was the one who got under my skin with all her stupid remarks about my (then) nonexistent love life. But now that I was the recent beneficiary of a lot of quality experience, I could turn the tables on her.

In a way I felt like I'd turned the tables on Henry, too, although that isn't the best way to say it. What I mean is that Henry and I seemed to have exchanged places in some ways. Not too long ago, I was the one staying home while Henry was seeing Celia. But now that he and Celia had broken up, Henry was the one perfecting the fine art of hanging out alone.

For just a minute we caught each other's eyes, and then Henry looked away.

"So," I said a little too loudly, "I'll see you guys later." I took the hearse keys out of a kitchen drawer where Mom keeps really important stuff like expired pizza coupons, and then I let myself out the back door.

Henry and I hadn't talked since the night we went running. We'd say stuff to each other like do you need a ride or isn't Fritz an idiot. But we didn't really talk.

I'd been thinking about the subject of silence lately and how many different kinds of silences there are. There's the kind of silence you feel on a date with a girl you don't know very well—the kind where things are so quiet that you can actually hear yourself sweat. Then there's the comfortable kind of silence you feel when you're around your family and best friends—people you've known so long that you don't have to say anything to each other. And finally there's the kind of silence that just covers things up. Silence like snow, making everything cold and white and totally unlike itself.

There was a whole canyon of that kind of silence between Henry and me right now. He was standing on one side and I was standing on the other. I hated it. But I was afraid that if I yelled out to him, all of it would come out—the anger, the feeling of betrayal, the hurt.

Especially the hurt.

I picked Diana up and we drove down to the lake

together. We did not, however, exchange pointers on kissing, or on anything else for that matter. We just sat there and listened to the radio for a while. One thing about me. I always know how to show a girl a good time.

"Why don't we just drive around for a while, Marcus?" Diana finally said.

I nodded, started the engine, and took off.

Diana hung her arm out the open window. The air lifted her hair and the setting sun made it glow so that she looked like she had a ring of fire around her head. "It's going to be warm tonight," she said.

"On nights like these," I told her, "Crazy Smitty takes off his pants and walks around the theater in his boxer shorts."

Diana laughed. I looked at her and smiled a little.

We drove toward town, passing beneath the viaduct that Henry, Frank, and I had run beneath the day we first met Frank. The same words were still there— the ones spray-painted in black that said WHY DOES IT HAVE TO HURT SO BAD?

The words started running through my head like some stupid line from a TV commercial you'd just as soon forget. Why does it have to hurt so bad, why does it have to hurt so bad—

"Let's stop over there." Diana pointed in the direction of Pioneer Park. It's a park here in town with a bandstand and swings and an old log cabin built by the first Mormon pioneers. The cabin has been restored and is open to visitors in the summer.

I rolled the hearse into the parking lot and Diana

and I got out. A hedge of lilac bushes was growing on the banks of a canal that runs through the park. The scent made me feel—I don't know—sad, I guess.

I took Diana's hand and we walked through the park.

"Have you ever been inside the cabin?" Diana asked.

"Once when I was a little kid. It's so small, it gave me the creeps."

Diana and I walked up and looked through the windows. We both had to stoop way down low just to get a look. I think you had to be a midget before they let you be a pioneer in those days. It was getting darker and harder to see. Still, we could make out a bed in the corner, a wooden table, and a couple of chairs. That was it. It was pretty hard to believe a whole entire family lived there once.

"I wonder where they kept their VCR," I said. Diana slugged me in the arm.

Not far from the cabin was a bronze statue that had turned green over the years. Around its base were the words IN MEMORY OF THOSE WHO LOST THEIR LIVES IN THE WARS AGAINST THE INDIANS.

Diana took her finger and traced a line down the bumpy list of names.

"Look, Marcus," she said. "Here's somebody named Jenkins. Just like you." She looked at me quickly, then said, "Things have changed a lot over the years, haven't they?"

I just kept staring at the statue, and then I said, "Guess what Coach Donahue told me today. Frank is coming back to Wakara High next year. His mama is making him. Don't you love it?"

Diana turned her full attention on me now. "I don't care what Frank does. I do care about you and Henry. You've got to fix whatever's wrong between you before he leaves next week."

"Me? I'm the one who's supposed to fix it? I'm not the party who wants to leave."

My hands started to shake. I shoved them into my pockets.

"I don't think he wants to leave. There are just some things he needs to figure out for himself," said Diana.

"He's never had to figure this stuff out before. So he's a Navaho. Big deal. Big stinking deal."

"It's a big deal to Henry. And I think it should be."

"I'll tell you what I think, Diana," I said, and my voice sounded angry in my own ears. "I think Henry's afraid. He split up with Celia. He got beat by Frank. He isn't top of the heap anymore. He can't take it, and now he's running away."

"Oh, Marcus—"

I went on. "Henry's running away from his problems here. But look where he's going. He's running to a place where there are a million guys just like Frank. He won't fit in. How could he? He told me himself that he feels white. They'll hate him."

"How do *you* know?"

"I just know." As soon as the words were out of my mouth, I realized how stupid they sounded. "I know everything. Just like Mr. Wizard."

Diana laughed softly, then grew serious again. "I think Henry knows more about what he's going back to than you do, Marcus." She stooped over to pick a flower growing at the base of the statue. She took my hand out of my pocket and dropped the flower on my palm. "It would mean a lot to him if he knew you supported him."

"He's going to leave whether I like it or not." My throat felt as thick as paste and my eyes started to sting. "I guess I just want to know why we can't give him what he needs. Why aren't we enough to keep him here?"

Diana didn't answer. I could stand in the park and ask my questions all night long and there wouldn't be any answers. Only the smell of lilacs and the sound of cars passing.

18

HENRY LEFT THE DAY after school got out.

I don't know. Maybe if I'd begged him to stick around for at least a week or so—just long enough to go boating and waterskiing a couple of times—he might have stayed with us at least that much longer for old times' sake. But I for sure didn't beg. I didn't even ask.

Henry went to the bus depot by himself. He told my parents he wanted it that way so that he didn't have to say good-bye again. Actually, I think he was afraid that everybody—Mom, Dad, Julia, Diana— would show up at the depot to send him off. Everybody but me. I guess he didn't want to have to face that.

So while Henry was sitting in the bus depot waiting to go back to the reservation on the first day of summer vacation, I was sitting on my bed making one of my lists. Only it was a regular boring list filled with regular boring things.

Stupid Stuff I Have to Do Today

1. *Mow lawn.*
2. *Weed.*
3. *Water geraniums.*
4. *Hose hearse.*
5. *Clean room.*

I heard the doorbell ring downstairs. A minute later Diana came bursting through my bedroom door.

"Hi," I said.

Diana was breathless. "Henry's bus leaves in half an hour," she said, gulping for air.

"I know." Then I shrugged.

"Well?"

I just gave her the look that I always give Mom when she wants me to do something totally against my principles, such as vacuuming my side of the bedroom. It says, *Hey, can't you see I'm busy mutating here?*

"Stop giving me that stupid look," said Diana, still breathing hard. She was also trembling because she was getting mad. For a minute there she looked just like the old Diana.

So I just kept staring at her, which is another technique I have for driving Mom crazy when I want to. I keep my mouth shut when she expects me to say something.

"Fine," Diana snapped. "Just sit here and feel sorry for yourself." She spun around and stormed out of my bedroom.

"Hey, wait a minute," I yelled after her. I jumped

off my bed. "I really resent that. I do *not* feel sorry for myself."

I ran out of my bedroom and into the hallway. Diana was already halfway down the staircase.

Clearly I had no choice. What else could I do but follow her?

Diana was waiting for me in the hearse by the time I found my keys. We didn't talk. I started the hearse and rolled out onto the street.

We had been driving for five minutes or so when suddenly Diana started to laugh.

"What's so funny?"

"I'm sorry I yelled at you," she said when she stopped laughing, "but when you gave me that *look* . . ." Then she started to laugh all over again.

I had to laugh myself. "That look always makes my mom crazy too. I guess she didn't learn about it in her Abnormal Kid Psychology class."

Diana kept on laughing. I reached across the seat for her hand.

"You never used to apologize for screaming at me," I told her. "And you used to scream at me all the time. Once you even told me that I babble."

"Did I really?" She moved closer to me and put her head on my shoulder. "Well, I guess things change sometimes, don't they?"

I didn't say anything for a minute, just sat there feeling Diana breathe. "Yeah," I said more to myself than to her, "I guess they do."

Sun was streaming through the windshield and the light made my eyes sting. I pulled down the visor to block the glare. Henry's sunglasses came tumbling out and dropped straight into my lap.

Henry had forgotten his sunglasses.

I had to smile to myself. Henry hardly ever forgets things. I stared at them for a second, then I picked the glasses up and stuffed them into my T-shirt pocket. Good thing Henry Yazzie had someone like me to help him out now and then.

The depot was practically empty when Diana and I got there—just a few employees standing around looking bored and Henry sitting on a wooden bench, staring out a plate-glass window. Except for Lazarus, who was meowing loudly in a cat carrier by Henry's feet, Henry was completely alone. Something about the sight of Henry sitting all by himself on a hard bench staring at nothing—it really got to me.

That night when we ran together was the first time I'd seen Henry's loneliness and I had taken it as a personal insult. But now I just felt sorry. Not for Henry. You'd never in a million years feel pity for a guy like Henry. But I did feel sorry for how much he hurt.

"Henry!" Diana called. Her voice bounced across the tile floors.

He turned his head quickly and saw us. For just a second he looked like he couldn't believe his eyes. And then he smiled.

Diana ran across the depot. Henry stood up to greet her.

"Diana!" He was still smiling. "I thought you'd be glad to get rid of me."

Diana pulled herself up straight. "Well, that's the meanest thing you've ever said to me. Don't you know when I make a friend, I make a friend for life? Even if he always does disagree with me."

"I'll miss our . . . discussions," Henry said. He laughed. "They've always been very enlightening."

Diana smiled. Suddenly she grabbed Henry's hand and kissed the tips of his fingers. Then she pressed his hand to her face.

Henry took her chin and turned her face so that he could look straight into it.

"Do you know what? You have beautiful eyes, Diana. I hope Marcus tells you that sometimes."

"Please take care of yourself, Henry," Diana murmured. Henry let go of her. Then he turned and looked at me.

I reached into my pocket and took out Henry's sunglasses. "Hey, Dr. Doom," I said. "You forgot these."

I handed him the glasses. Henry took them.

"So I did," he said. "So I did." Then he put them on.

I laughed.

The two of us stood there for a moment, just staring at each other like we were two kids again meeting each other for the first time. When I looked at Henry, I wondered what his Navaho grandfather looked like. Maybe he looked just like Henry, only older.

I thought about what his grandfather had said about different worlds being layered on top of each other and how there were stars in the spaces between the worlds.

Well, I guess there are all kinds of ways of seeing things. Some people like me look at the sky and just see stars. Other people like Henry's grandfather look at the sky and see—I don't know what. Roads, maybe. Leading to other worlds.

"Hey, good luck, Doctor," I said finally. "Get your rear back here in the fall where it belongs. Come back to us like you did that first time." And then I added something I hadn't planned on saying. "But only if you can." I put out my hand. Henry grabbed it, his grip as tight as a vise.

"Brothers?" he said. There was a question in his voice. A little one. But it was still there.

You know how people who nearly die say they see their whole lives flash before their eyes? Well, that happened to me right there in the middle of the bus depot. My life with Henry flashed before my eyes. I saw Henry and me at the theater, in the hearse, at Celia's house, in Miss Brett's classroom. I saw us running, taking the garbage out, teasing Julia, helping Diana fish Lazarus out of the Dumpster. I heard us laughing and talking and bugging Dad about his stupid music and swearing and shooting the bull. And I saw Henry and me, two little kids with funny haircuts, dragging our sleeping bags out onto the lawn at night so that Henry could see the stars.

"Brothers," I told him. My own grip tightened around Henry's hand. *"Always!"*

Epilogue

I THOUGHT OF THAT POEM Miss Brett made us read. The one that began with the line "When you are old . . ." I even looked it up and read it again.

> When you are old and gray and full of sleep,
> And nodding by the fire, take down this book,
> And slowly read, and dream of the soft look
> Your eyes had once, and of their shadows deep;
>
> How many loved your moments of glad grace,
> And loved your beauty, with love false or true;
> But one man loved the pilgrim soul in you,
> And loved the sorrows of your changing face.
> —William Butler Yeats

I know it's supposed to be just a love poem—an old guy writing to a lady he still loves—but I sort of think the poem describes *life* in general. Everything in life changes. Everything. Seasons, styles, the town you grew up in, the people you know, even the way you feel about all the people you know. All those things change. In fact, change is about the only thing you can really count on. Still, it's like Diana said the night I first heard her sing. You can still *decide* to care. You can decide to love someone even though they've changed. Maybe you can even learn to love them because of it. Does any of that make sense?

I've started running at night now—just like Henry used to. Like Henry, I'm not the world's greatest letter writer, so this is my strange little way of keeping in touch with him. I run the same course we ran together that spring night. I run to the mouth of the canyon and back. Now that it's summer, the fruit trees are covered with leaves and tiny unripe apples. When the hot July sun hits them in the morning, the leaves burn bright green.

When I run I like to think that Henry's running somewhere, too, late at night out in the desert, that rock-rimmed world of his where I don't belong. I hope that he's running straight and strong toward whatever it is he wants to find and that the ghost at his heels is gone.

On clear bright nights like this one I can see him in my mind's eye, running across the desert's red dirt with the moon in his eyes.

And the stars in his hair.

S.E. HINTON

☐ **TAMING THE STAR RUNNER**   20479-8 $3.50
Travis and the Star Runner are two of a kind—free spirits not meant to be tamed.

☐ **THE OUTSIDERS**   96769-4 $3.25
The instant classic about a gang from the wrong side of the tracks. A major motion picture starring Matt Dillon.

☐ **RUMBLE FISH**   97534-4 $3.50
Tough guy Rusty James would kill to be like his brother, Motorcycle Boy—the most respected hood in town. A major motion picture starring Matt Dillon.

☐ **TEX**   97850-5 $3.50
Bronc-and-bike-happy Tex doesn't have a care in the world—until he learns a secret about his drifter dad that changes his life forever. A major motion picture starring Matt Dillon.

☐ **THAT WAS THEN, THIS IS NOW**   98652-4 $3.50
Byron and Mark are closer than brothers...until Bryon discovers that Mark is dealing drugs! A major motion picture starring Emilio Estevez.

DATE DUE

S.B.-1